Crackaway's Quest

It is almost two years since Custer's defeat at the Little Bighorn and apart from those few who have followed Sitting Bull into Canada, the Sioux have been chased out of the Black Hills and are now subjugated by life on a reservation. But rumours of unrest and a renewal of hostilities are causing concern among the people of the northern settlements. The arrival of a buckskin-clad stranger with eagle feathers affixed to his hat and the mane of his pony is greeted with curiosity and caution by the people of Palmersville. The violence that ensues when he voices sympathy for the plight of the tribes people might have been avoided if his attackers had first learned his name. For the stranger is wagon train scout Wes Gray, known throughout the west as Medicine Feather, brother of the Arapaho and friend of the Sioux.

Crackaway's Quest

Will DuRey

A Black Horse Western

ROBERT HALE

© Will DuRey 2016
First published in Great Britain 2016

ISBN 978-0-7198-2100-4

The Crowood Press
The Stable Block
Crowood Lane
Ramsbury
Marlborough
Wiltshire SN8 2HR

www.bhwesterns.com

Robert Hale is an imprint
of The Crowood Press

Typeset by
Derek Doyle & Associates, Shaw Heath
Printed and bound in Great Britain by
CPI Group (UK) Ltd, Croydon, CR0 4YY

ONE

The afternoon sun was still high when the man rode into town on the long-backed pinto. Both man and beast were dust covered and looked tired, as though they'd journeyed far to reach this settlement. The man was tall, broad across the shoulders and had a long, expressionless face. He was dressed in fringed buckskin and wore soft moccasins on his feet. His brown, felt hat had a wide brim and a long eagle feather had been fixed securely into the colourful band around its crown. A necklace of coloured stones sat tightly around his thick neck and the doeskin pouch which housed the long-gun he carried across his saddle was splendidly fringed and carefully decorated with the finest designs of the Arapaho people. As he rode, he studied those curious, perhaps cautious faces that were turned in his direction. He had the distinct impression that there was little welcome for him here.

5

Any hint of recent contact with Indians was endorsed by the beast beneath him. Although harnessed with a white-man's saddle, it walked like the pony of an Indian scout; its neck outstretched, its head low and its feet set down softly, like those of a stalking cougar with the scent of a wary pronghorn in its nostrils. The pinto might have looked exhausted but its ears were pricked upright, proving that it was alert to its new surroundings. Not only was it interested in the smells of the town but it was wary, too, of the new sounds and sights. With each careful stride, muscles rippled from its deep chest to its solid back haunches, decrying its lethargic appearance and denoting to any keen judge of horseflesh its ability to produce sustained bursts of speed. It awaited only the rider's command to leave this town far behind. That command didn't come; instead it was guided towards the hitching rail outside the Silver Nugget where the man dismounted.

Palmersville wasn't a big town, in fact, until the discovery of silver two years earlier, it hadn't been a town at all, merely the site of a trading post whose importance had diminished since the near demise of the beaver trade. But now there was a street of timber buildings that housed the necessities of civilisation; doctor, undertaker, barber, emporium and barroom. The latter was the biggest establishment, the one that every man in town would have entered most regularly. The man pushed against the batwing doors and went inside.

It was a big room but dingy, as though it had been built on the wrong side of the street to prohibit sunlight from shining directly through its windows, but there were low-hanging kerosene lamps to provide the necessary illumination for the card players, roulette gamblers and chuck-a-luck gamesters who would fill the place at the end of the working day. For now, only a handful of men were inside, most of them occupied the window tables where there was enough natural light to see a companion's face. The barman was a stocky fellow, a couple of inches below average height but as rotund as one of his beer barrels. He wore a hard expression on his face, signifying that he was as tough as he needed to be to run a successful frontier beer palace. He had no facial hair and not a lot on top, either. He wore a fancy waistcoat over a white shirt and a slim black tie around his neck. Anticipating the man's needs, he reached behind and grabbed a bottle from the shelf under the long mirror before speaking.

'What'll it be?'

'A cold beer if you have one.'

'I've got beer,' the barman said, letting the bottle he'd reached for settle back in its position on the back counter, 'but I can't guarantee the temperature. Ran out of ice a week ago. Two bits if you want it.'

The buckskin-clad newcomer dug into a pocket for some coins while the barman poured the contents of a bottle transported from a St Louis Brewery into a thick glass. Half the contents were quaffed in one swallow. It was the man's first beer for almost six months. The last had been when he'd parted company with wagonmaster Caleb Dodge in California and then ridden north to winter with his wife's Arapaho people along the Snake River. This beer was too warm to be good but it washed away the journey's dust and left a hint of what awaited him in Council Bluffs where the saloons were equipped with better storage facilities than were available in this remote mining town.

'New in town?' the barman asked, and when the stranger answered with a nod, posed another question. 'Just passing through?'

The stranger's grey-eyed stare pierced the barman. It was an unwritten code throughout the west that a man's business was his own and it didn't pay to pry too deeply.

'No offence meant,' the barman said, 'but you don't look like you're here to grub for silver.'

'That's right,' the stranger told him, then downed the beer that remained in the glass.

'You been west of here? In the Black Hills? There's talk of trouble with the Sioux. Just wondering if you'd seen any sign.'

'Those that aren't in Canada with Sitting Bull are on reservations. There's no trouble with the Sioux or any other tribe in this territory.'

'Still a few hostile bands roving the high ground and attacking isolated farms,' insisted the barman.

The stranger shook his head. 'That's not true. Perhaps a cow or two has been stolen in the night but not by war parties. More likely the work of an individual warrior trying to feed his family.'

'You talk like you're on their side.'

The gruff barman's voice attracted the attention of a couple of men at the far end of the bar who turned with unfriendly scowls on their faces. Their clothing wasn't redolent of mine-workers, more the apparel of range riders. One wore black trousers, a rough red shirt and a black hat; the other wore denim trousers, a black shirt topped by a short jacket and a grey hat. The stranger noted their interest but was neither looking for trouble nor keen to get involved in a discussion about the rights and wrongs of the government's Indian policies. In his opinion, the changes demanded of the tribespeople were too much, too soon. It would take time, perhaps another generation or more before they could begin to adapt successfully to the culture of the Americans. Even then, it would only be achieved if they were treated with honesty and goodwill. But for now, the fighting was finished, that was a good starting point. So his reply was meant to placate any anger that seemed to be simmering among the men in the room. 'Just stating a fact. Leave the Sioux alone and they'll keep to the reservation.'

One of the men, the red shirt, pushed himself away from the counter, drew himself to his full height which was no less than the stranger's six feet. He inspected the newcomer's attire, taking special interest in the long feather in the newcomer's hat. To his friend's amusement, he said derisively, 'You look like you belong on a reservation yourself.'

All other conversations in the room had ceased; everyone was listening to the talk at the counter. The barman's eyes shifted warily to the left, as though the two had a history of causing trouble on his premises.

It wasn't the first time the stranger had been singled out in a new town. His appearance had got him into more fights than he cared to remember but he had no plans to discard the buckskins. When he rode west again, when he was crossing the continent with Caleb Dodge's wagon train, the tough wearing clothes outlasted anything he could buy in the mercantile stores of the east. So, for now, he was prepared to ignore the man's goading. 'I'm looking for a man called Crackaway,' he told the barman. 'Do you know where I can find him?'

It was the man along the bar who spoke in response. Again his voice full of disdain, as though believing the stranger was afraid of him because he'd refused to respond to the previous taunt. 'That drunken old coot,' he said. 'Should have known you and he were partners. You carry the same dirty smell of Indians.'

With startling suddenness, the stranger turned to face the jeering man, the expression on his bronzed face as terrible as any depiction of blood-thirsty savages in a penny dreadful, and the cold stare of his ice-grey eyes froze the leer on the other's face. When he took a step forward his agitator took steps to defend himself, his right hand dropping towards the butt of his holstered pistol.

The barman said, 'No fighting in here,' but with a tone that implied he had no expectation of his demand being observed.

The stranger growled at his opponent. 'Touch that gun and I'll kill you.'

The man stilled his hand, his previous aggression shattered by the certainty that his opponent was capable of fulfilling his threat. He watched with unblinking eyes as the other approached.

The stranger began talking, declaring that not only did he have friends among the Sioux but he also had a Sioux wife. 'When you insult them you insult me. Next time I'll. . . .' The stranger didn't finish his sentence, his eyes suddenly stung by whiskey that had been thrown by the second man. Half hidden by his companion, he had flung the contents of his whiskey glass and now, while their adversary was rubbing the liquid from his eyes, followed up with the whiskey bottle which he was holding by the neck.

The stranger had been fighting all his life; he knew as much about barroom tactics as he did about military tactics in war. He reacted instantly, grabbing the wrist of the arm that was descending towards his head and twisting with as much violence as he could generate. The man yelled and turned in an effort to free himself of the pain. He dropped the bottle, which smashed on the floor and the stranger released him, pushing him so that he collided with his partner.

Red shirt's former bravado had been restored by

his companion's attack and, sensing they were about to gain the upper hand in the affray, reached for his gun. When his companion crashed into him he was hurled backwards on to the floor, his weapon sliding away across the room. Anxiously, he looked around for it, spotted it under a table and, seeing that the stranger was re-grappling with his friend, began to scuttle across the floor to collect it. He hated to admit it, but he'd been more frightened for his life in the past few moments than he'd ever known before, chilled by the expression on the frontiersman's face. It was an experience he hadn't enjoyed and didn't want to repeat. If he got the opportunity to kill the stranger he would take it.

The buckskin-clad man had hoped that the fight would come to an end when he took away the bottle, but that hope soon vanished when he saw red shirt attempt to draw his gun. For the moment though, red shirt was on the floor and separated from his weapon – it was the first man who was the major threat. He was on his feet, armed and as full of murderous intent as his companion. In order to prevent him from drawing his gun, the stranger hurled himself forward. He threw a low, left arm hook that struck the man in the solar plexus, doubling him over and making his jaw an open target for a vicious, downward right-hand punch. The man in the grey hat dropped to his knees and his body would have stretched its length on the floor if the stranger hadn't grabbed his shirt with his left hand and held his head up to enable another right-hand punch to be delivered. Then he let the senseless man drop.

By this time, the man in the red shirt was slithering under a table to reach his gun. The stranger raced across the room, casting aside chairs and overturning a table in his haste. Just as his opponent's fingers were about to settle on the gun handle, the stranger grabbed his legs and pulled him away. Instinct was the source of red shirt's resistance and as he was being dragged across the floor he grasped the leg of a chair and hurled it at his opponent. It struck its target, one leg connecting with a cheekbone just below the eye. The man released his hold for an instant and his adversary came up off the floor, pulling a knife from a sheath as he did so.

'I'm going to gut you,' he snarled but it was a prediction with little chance of success. His chest-high swipe was easily evaded by the lithe, buckskin-clad figure who then took two steps back and put a table between them, giving himself time to draw his own weapon, a big hunting knife that hung down his left thigh. He hefted it from right hand to left then back again, letting his opponent know that he was accustomed to using the weapon, that he was skilful and deadly.

Red shirt swiped again, the impetus almost making him fall forward on to the table. Before fully regaining his balance, the stranger grasped the edge of the table and pushed, forcing his opponent to retreat until he was trapped against the back wall. Angry, desperate, casting caution aside, red shirt slashed again and again without success.

While the knife was at the highest point of its arc, the stranger struck, smashing the butt-end of the bone handle of his own knife against red shirt's temple. With an ugly, pain-filled yell, he slumped forward on to the table. The stranger took the knife from his enemy's hand, dropped it on the floor near the pistol then pressed the man's head against the table and put the point of his hunting knife to his throat. He could hear the man's breath rasping horribly in his throat. His eyes bulged horribly at the prospect of death.

The stranger had no intention of killing the vanquished man but wanted him to know that, if he chose, he had the power to do so. He wanted to find the words that would put an end to the intolerance which was the biggest obstacle to a lasting peace with the tribes, but he couldn't even explain to himself how the few minutes he'd spent in this town had brought him to being within a thrust of taking another man's life. He'd done so with similar provocation in the past, but he wouldn't this day. He was in Palmersville merely to meet his old friend Crackaway and had no desire to be detained here because of other men's prejudices. There were wagons assembled at Council Bluffs and a wagonmaster waiting for him to guide them west. Even while that thought was in his head, a gun butt cracked against his skull and he dropped into unconsciousness.

When he opened his eyes he was lying on a bunk and confronted by a line of iron bars. He moved, tried to sit upright and groaned with the effort. Holding his head in his hands, he sat on the edge of the low bed. Somewhere from the other side of the bars a chair creaked and footsteps approached. The man who hovered into his view was broad and grey and had a star pinned to his shirt.

'Take your time,' the sheriff said. 'People move too quickly after taking a heavy blow and they're likely to spew. Can't abide the smell and I daresay you don't relish the prospect of swilling out the jailhouse.'

'Who hit me?' asked the stranger.

'I did,' the sheriff told him. 'Didn't want you shoving that great blade through Carter's neck. He's not the town's most prestigious citizen but I'd have been obliged to hang you for murder if you'd gone through with it.'

'I wasn't going to kill him,' the stranger mumbled.

'Only got your word for that.' He threw another sentence over his shoulder as he walked back towards his desk. 'Come on out when your head clears, the door's open.'

'If I'm not under arrest what was I doing in one of your cells?' the stranger asked when he joined the sheriff in the outer office.

'Arresting you was my intention when I cracked your head open but when I asked around it became clear that you'd been acting in your own defence. Didn't take a lot of deductive power to identify the aggressor. Carter's gun was across the room but yours was still in your holster, which tends to support your statement that you didn't intend killing him. Besides,

Benny Kingston at the saloon told me that Carter had been the first one to pull a knife. He's a mean fighter. You did well to best him. What's your name?'

'Wes Gray.'

The sheriff looked at the stranger with renewed interest. 'Wes Gray! The same Wes Gray that some people call Medicine Feather?'

'That's me.'

'Well, I guess Tad Carter was a lucky man. It also explains the cause of your fight. Benny Kingston said you were arguing about Indians.'

Wes Gray didn't respond. He'd seen his hat and gunbelt on a rack near the door and his Winchester in its fringed pouch propped against the wall below them. He stepped over to retrieve them.

The sheriff spoke again. 'People around town are jumpy at present. There's talk of fresh hostilities. They remember the raids that took place in the past. Some of them lost kinsfolk so they don't have much sympathy with the plight of the Indians nor take kindly to people who do.'

'Nothing for folks to be concerned about. The Sioux have moved on to reservation land. What more can they do?'

'A more important question is will they stay there? There are rumours that the braves are discontent with their treatment, that the supplies that are being allotted to them are substandard and insufficient for their needs. They are threatening to break out of the reservation to hunt for what they want. If it's true then it's only right to assume they'll steal livestock from the

16

surrounding farms which will lead to fighting and killing.'

Wes finished buckling the belt before speaking. 'Do you place much trust in these rumours, Sheriff?'

'Well, they aren't being denied by the people who deal with the Indians.'

'Like who, for instance?'

'John Lord. His men drive the cattle that arrive at the Spearpoint railhead up to the Agency buildings on the reservation. It's prime stock they get. I've been at Spearpoint when the trucks have been unloaded. But the Indians complain. It's as if they're looking for an excuse to go raiding again.'

Wes Gray put a different interpretation on the rumour. In his opinion it was more likely that vicious white men were conjuring up an excuse to attack the near-defenceless Indians on their reservation. For the moment he could only hope that they were both wrong and that the rumours would peter out without resulting in bloodshed. 'I came to town to meet a friend,' he told the sheriff. 'Goes by the name Crackaway. Have you seen him?'

The lawman rubbed at his jaw. 'I've seen him. Been hanging around town for a few days. Drunk most of the time or sleeping it off in his room at Mrs Trantor's place. Don't know how she's put up with him.'

Wes Gray had known Crackaway for many years. They'd trapped together in the Powder River country before the War between the States, had spent two winters in a cabin in the Rockies and had bumped into each other in unlikely settlements across the west.

17

Wes had come to Palmersville in response to a message that Crackaway had sent. There were no details, but Crackaway wouldn't have sent for him if it hadn't been important. 'Where is Mrs Trantor's place?'

'Among the buildings behind the bank. Her house has a swing on the porch. But you won't find Crackaway there today. He's up at the cemetery. We buried him yesterday.'

A deep furrowed scowl settled on Wes Gray's face. 'What happened?' he asked.

'Don't know for sure. Got into an argument with the horses at the livery stable. They were probably offended by the reek of whiskey.' The sheriff paused, remembered he was talking to a friend of the dead man and continued with more compassion. 'He was found by the stableman one morning. He'd been trampled to death.'

'What was he doing in the stable?'

'Nobody knows. Probably stumbled in there to sleep off the whiskey.'

Wes tried to worm more details out of the sheriff but without success. According to the lawman, no one knew where the old man had come from, nor his purpose for being in Palmersville. He had no friends, no special acquaintance so the reason for the summons was in danger of being an unsolved mystery.

'I suppose you'll be riding on now,' said the sheriff.

'Not tonight.' Wes rubbed his head to show he was still carrying the after-effects of the blow he'd received. 'Where will I get a bed?'

'If you're not squeamish, don't mind sleeping in a dead man's bed, I reckon Mrs Trantor has a vacancy.'

TWO

The three horsemen had ridden past the sheriff's office half a minute earlier and therefore didn't see Wes Gray when he stepped outside. At walking pace, they proceeded along the main street, looking neither right nor left but exuding a certain amount of arrogance which seemed to carry with it an unspoken threat. One man, astride a high black, was three-quarters of a length ahead of the other two, his back straight like an army general riding through conquered enemy territory. Few townspeople looked in his direction. No one hailed him with a greeting. When they reached the last buildings, they pricked their horses into a canter and left the town behind.

Wes Gray had watched them until they were out of sight. The two men who had been riding like guardsmen to their commander were the two with whom he'd fought in the saloon. Their absence from town, if it overlapped his departure in the morning, satisfied him. He'd be happy to quit Palmersville without arousing any more trouble. As he walked down the street, however, the sheriff's assessment of the mood of the townspeople was instantly apparent to him. Openly, they watched him with a mixture of mistrust and contempt, attributable, he could only suppose, to the manner of his appearance. In themselves, buck-skin clothes were not extraordinary in this territory, but his distinctive Indian stone necklace and the long eagle feather in his hat were unquestionably responsi-ble for the angry glares he was attracting. He was a stranger to the town, unknown to the residents, and in such a small settlement word of his spirited defence of the Indian peoples would have spread rapidly.

Three things prevented him from climbing on to the back of the pinto that remained hitched to the rail outside the saloon. First, he'd anticipated a night in a soft bed and now, following the blow on the head from the sheriff's gun butt, it was an even more pleas-ant prospect. His discomfort wouldn't be eased sitting astride his beast.

The second consideration that prevented him leaving town was stubbornness. He wasn't prepared to be forced out by the animosity of the townspeople. He had done nothing wrong. His interpretation of the sit-uation might vary from theirs but it was no less valid. He had no plan to confront anyone with his views but he wouldn't shirk from stating them if it became nec-essary. The transition from nomadic hunter to settled farmer would not be easy for the tribespeople. Understanding and tolerance would be required if the government's reservation policy was to succeed, but he was aware that the mental scars of the pioneer families were as deep as any inflicted by axe-blade, arrow or scalping knife.

The last reason for not riding clear of Palmersville was a deep-seated need to know Crackaway's reason for bringing him here. His curiosity was piqued by the description of a whiskey-guzzling sot as supplied by both the sheriff and Carter with whom he'd fought. Crackaway had been fond of the jug, a fact that Wes couldn't deny, but the old man had a head as hard as iron and could hold his liquor as well as any man he'd ever known. People change, but only something drastic could have transposed Crackaway into a town drunk. But he hadn't been too drunk to forget Wes's springtime route to Council Bluffs and leave a message for him twenty miles north, where the White River converged with the Missouri.

As he hefted his long rifle into the crook of his left arm his first thought was to find a bed for the night. Saloons usually weren't fussy about the people who occupied their upstairs rooms and were usually cheaper than those establishments which carried the title hotel, but Palmersville had only one saloon and he'd already made himself known there and caused damage. If Carter or his friend came looking for revenge it was the first place they'd seek him out. He wasn't afraid to face them, just wary of becoming embroiled in a feud that might delay his journey to Council Bluffs and his rendezvous there with Caleb Dodge and the westbound wagons. The sheriff's suggestion appealed, but there were drawbacks to using a boarding house. Usually they weren't interested in taking a lodger for only one night and they were more particular who they let across their threshold. If his reputation had reached the ears of Mrs Trantor she might have a prejudice against people who consorted with Indians.

He paused by the bank, a low, uninspiring building of thin timbers that looked to be the least secure building in the small town. Casting a look down the lane that ran away from the main street, Wes could see the collection of buildings among which would be Mrs Trantor's boarding house. He had been in few frontier towns that didn't draw heavy-drinking, argumentative gambling men to their main streets after dark and although small, he had no hesitation in supposing that Palmersville was no different. Whether the neighbourhood was predominantly populated by cattle drovers or miners, the magnets of liquor, cards and women never failed to work. The more peaceful environs away from the main street and saloon would, Wes thought, be more conducive to a good night's sleep. He resolved to seek a bed at Mrs Trantor's house; she could do no worse than refuse. Still, he didn't immediately turn off the main thoroughfare. He had another visit to make first. His only reason for being in Palmersville was to meet up with his old companion, Crackaway. It behoved him therefore to walk up to the cemetery to see where he was he lying.

The cemetery was located about a quarter-mile beyond the livery stable and blacksmith's shop which were the last buildings on the town's western extremity.

Wes Gray had passed it on his arrival. Beyond, tall poles that marked the entrance of the white-railed graveyard could be clearly seen. Wes headed for them with a long, easy stride.

His approach was noted by the smith, who was smiting with his hammer just inside the timber-frame building that was his forge. Beneath his leather apron he was bare-chested, his skin gleamed with sweat and was smudged with smoke. He paused in his work as though hopeful that the buckskin-clad figure was bringing business his way but when it became apparent that the town's newcomer was not stopping he stepped outside and cast a look in the direction of his destination. He could see the three horsemen who had ridden past only moments earlier. They were at a standstill, gathered near the cemetery gates, waiting for something or someone.

'Mister,' he called to Wes Gray, 'got a minute?'

'What's on your mind?'

The smith inclined his head towards the distant horsemen. 'If you're heading up to the cemetery you might want to let Lord and his men finish their business first. They'll be riding on in a minute or two. Nothing to gain by further antagonism.'

The smith's words now identified for Wes the third member of the trio, John Lord, a name he'd already heard. The far man, dressed in a black wool coat, black hat and sitting motionless astride a fine black horse reminded Wes Gray of sculptures he'd seen in the east, erected to the memory of war-time heroes. Positioned as he was outside the gates of Palmersville cemetery, John Lord, it seemed, was a monument to death.

The smith spoke again. 'Heard you got the best of Carter and Oates in the saloon. Perhaps you weren't lucky. Perhaps you'd whip them again in a fair fight, but they are mean men, they won't care what tricks they use to get their revenge.'

'Obliged for the warning,' Wes told him, 'but I'm not looking for trouble and there's no reason to suppose they're waiting up there for me. I didn't know I was heading this way myself until my feet brought me here. No need for their business to interfere with mine.'

'No need,' the smith agreed, 'but doesn't mean they won't go out of their way to make sure it does.'

'I'll deal with that if it becomes necessary,' Wes told him, and moved away to continue his walk up to the cemetery. He stopped then turned back to speak to the smith again. 'My horse is down the street. Can I stable him here for the night?'

The blacksmith pointed to the words painted over the high doors. 'Ask anyone hereabouts,' he told Wes, 'they'll tell you this is the best livery stable in town.' He grinned. It was probably a line he shot to every newcomer. Not only was it the only livery stable in town but the yellow-painted name read R. Best, Blacksmith. 'Fifty cents to leave him overnight, another fifty to comb and feed him.'

Wes told the man he would pay his dollar later, when he brought the pinto for stabling. Then he headed up the small incline to the graveyard, sure in the knowledge that the trio's reason for pausing there had no connection with him. When he was a hundred yards short of the gateway, three heads turned to watch his approach.

Carter manoeuvred his mount so that he was closer to John Lord, and although their verbal exchange was too quiet for Wes to hear, he reckoned he grasped the purport of their conversation. Carter was informing the other that Wes was the man he'd fought in the saloon and Lord, reaching across to rest his hand on Carter's gun hand, was insisting upon restraint. The haughtiness that Wes had detected earlier while watching Lord's progress along the main street was now more pronounced in the manner he sat with one arm cocked against his hip. His chin jutted under stern lips as though pointing at Wes like a hunting dog anxious to prove its superiority over its prey. There was an attempt to convey a placatory message when he spoke, but his gruff voice couldn't disguise an element of animosity.

'You're a friend to the red man, I understand,' he began.

'I know some,' answered Wes.

'Time to let the battles of the past slip into history. Bury the war-axe so to speak.'

'Do those men work for you?' Wes moved his head to indicate Carter and Oates.

'They do.'

'Then your observations would be better directed at them.'

'I heard that the three of you had had a disagreement

but you see, Mister. . . ?'

'Gray. Wes Gray.'

'Wes Gray! Well that's a name most people in this territory have heard.' He turned his head so that he could see the faces of his confederates.

It was clear that they, too, were aware of the reputation of the man they were confronting: Carter's face had lost a little of its colour, recalling how he'd been pinned to the table with a hunting knife at his throat. In the intervening time he'd made some brash remarks about the injuries he would have inflicted on the stranger if the sheriff hadn't interrupted the fight, and now the expression on Lord's face seemed to be egging him on to prove the worth of those comments.

'You've got to understand, Mr Gray,' said John Lord, 'the Indian wars have caused much suffering to the people around here.'

'I understand that, just as I understand the great suffering caused to the Indians. And I agree that there should be no more fighting, but that will only be achieved when the treaty agreements are upheld.'

'Well I don't know of any attempt to deprive the Indians of their due rations,' Lord said.

'Yeah,' chimed in Carter, feeling secure in the fact that they outnumbered Wes three-to-one, 'they're getting what they deserve.'

'I expect that one day you'll get what you deserve.' The icy-coldness both in Wes Gray's voice and his grey-eyed stare unsettled Carter once more. The words were more than a threat; they were a promise, the fulfilment of which would not inconvenience the frontiersman.

'You wouldn't be so brave if you didn't have your rifle in your hands,' muttered Carter as a patina of sweat showed on his brow.

Wes regarded the still covered long-gun that was cradled in his arms. 'You think I'd be prepared to shoot through the scabbard? It wouldn't be worth damaging it to kill you. But,' with a deft movement he twisted the rifle so that he was holding it at arm's length, its butt on the ground, 'if this makes things more even for you then make your move.'

Wes's right hand, free now of its hold on the long-gun, hovered close to the butt of the Colt that was holstered on his right thigh. His eyes were centred on Carter but the distance that separated him from the mounted trio was such that he was also able to watch for any aggressive movement from the other two. For a moment, two, all was still. Carter's eyes widened then narrowed as the prospect of gunplay edged towards inevitability. He wasn't a stranger to the practise, he had killed men face-to-face in the past, but they hadn't been men with such a reputation as that enjoyed by Wes Gray. He licked his lips and wondered if John Lord would intervene, would find an excuse that would defuse the situation. On reflection, he knew he had little expectation of intervention from that quarter. He recalled the look that his employer had thrown at him only moments earlier. It had been a mixture of humorous surprise that he'd escaped with his life and reckless encouragement to prove his

28

vaunted ability with a handgun. No doubt he also wanted to see how fast Wes Gray could draw, whether the stories that were told about him were true. No, there would be no reprieve; he had to go for his gun.

The rattle of wood on wood as the cemetery gate was closed behind the three horsemen distracted everyone. Immediately, John Lord rode his horse between Carter and Wes Gray to put an end to the threatened shoot-out. From behind the horses, a girl, a young woman, came into Wes Gray's view. She was tallish, with light brown hair piled on top of her head from which stray wisps teased around her ears and eyes. She brushed them aside as she walked. Mid-stride she paused, sensing that her arrival had impacted on an awkward situation. She wore a long grey skirt and matching small jacket over a white blouse. She looked at the horsemen and it seemed to Wes that her face registered anger when she recognized John Lord.

What began as a glance at Wes lingered long enough to give herself time to absorb the manner of his attire. Their eyes met for a brief moment; the woman's were as green as spring buffalo grass, made more spectacular by the sun-toned smooth skin in which they were set.

'Jenny,' John Lord said, 'I was waiting to speak to you.'

'You shouldn't have bothered.' The girl began to walk towards the buildings of Palmersville.

'It's important, Jenny. We have things to talk about.'

'No. We don't.'

John Lord turned and spoke to his men. 'Ride on,' he told them, 'I'll catch up shortly.'

The tension that had been created by the prospect of violence disappeared as Carter and Oates pulled at the reins of their horses to turn them on to the trail west. But Carter threw a look at Wes Gray that suggested that on another day there would be a letting of the bad blood that existed between them. Their enmity had arisen in an instant but would last until death. Wes re-cradled the rifle in the crook of his arm and set his sights on the gateway into the graveyard.

Twenty yards away, astride the black horse, John Lord was making another attempt to talk to the girl. 'Why are you being so obstructive?' he asked.

'Perhaps because I don't like you.' She was trying to work her way around the horse that he was using to obstruct her route back to town. Exasperated, she pushed against the horse's breast and dodged around the animal.

'I'll call tonight,' Lord insisted, 'and we'll discuss it in a sensible manner.'

'Don't bother,' snapped the young woman, who found herself confronted by the horse once more.

'Who else could you choose? No one within two hundred miles matches my wealth or influence.'

From up the trail, Wes Gray called, 'You have no influence over me nor, I suspect over the lady. She's made her position clear so I suggest you stop bothering her and catch up with your buddies.'

John Lord pulled his horse's head around then

spurred the animal up to where Wes Gray was standing. 'You might have a reputation for fighting savages but that doesn't give you any right to interfere in my affairs. My advice to you is to get back on your horse and get out of Palmersville at the earliest opportunity.'

'You might be wealthy but you don't own the town. I'll go when I'm ready and my advice to you is to leave that young woman alone.'

'What I do is no business of yours.'

'I'm making it my business. Stay away from her.'

John Lord made a movement towards his six-gun but arrested it before his hand reached the pistol's butt. He was looking down the long barrel of Wes Gray's Colt.

'Now ride,' Wes ordered and he remained at the graveyard gate until John Lord had put half a mile between them.

By that time, the girl was almost back to the best livery stable in Palmersville. Wes re-holstered his gun and went deeper into the cemetery. He found the fresh grave near the back rails. It seemed to be the place where the least wealthy were put to rest. A simple wooden plaque bore the legend *Crackaway Died 1878*. It wasn't much of an epitaph for a brave man, but a small bunch of violet flowers rested against the marker. Wes wondered who had shown that token of kindness.

THREE

The blacksmith ceased pumping the bellows and cast a silent, candid gaze at Weston Gray as he passed by on his return from the cemetery. It carried the message that he'd witnessed the confrontation at the graveyard gateway and approved of the outcome. Perhaps it also carried the hope that if the frontiersman hung around long enough he could bring about a lot of changes in Palmersville.

To Wes Gray's knowledge, Best's forge and livery was the only stable in town so the building he was passing had to be the place where Crackaway had died. He wondered if the blacksmith had been the one to discover the old man's body. Perhaps he would ask the big man what he knew about his friend's death, but that would keep until later. For now, his first task was to find a room for the night. He took the turning at the bank, immediately identified the property he was seeking and made a bee line for it.

The fence that surrounded Mrs Trantor's lodging house was freshly white, as was the paintwork around the windows and door. The rest of the woodwork was green and it, too, seemed to have been applied recently. There was a garden between the fence and the porch, which was packed with a variety of flowers that Wes couldn't identify. His knowledge of plants was restricted to those with medicinal value and those which he knew were dangerous to eat. He hadn't learned the names of those that were only for ornamentation. But his eyes were drawn to a row of small, purple, bell-shaped flowers growing at the foot of the veranda. They were identical to those that had been placed against Crackaway's graveyard marker. If Crackaway's landlady had been moved to mark his passing then the old man's liquor intake hadn't been as offensive to her as the sheriff had supposed.

A voice broke into his reverie. 'They were his favourite.'

Wes turned his attention to the porch. She was sitting on the swing, motionless, swallowed by the shadows that were lengthening as the sun slipped lower in the sky. Her feet were planted solidly on the wooden boards of the porch and the tips of black shoes showed below the hemline of her long grey skirt. Her hands were lightly clasped in her lap, a sign of contentment, as though she was at a Sunday Meeting after a good harvest had been gathered in.

'Crackaway's?'

'Yes,' she confirmed, 'Crackaway's.' Her voice was heavy with reflection, as though the death of the old man had greatly lessened her own existence.

'You put some on his grave.'

'The marker needed embellishment.'

'Yes ma'am. There was a lot more to Crackaway than a name and the year of his death.'

The woman turned and went inside the house. She paused in the doorway to assure herself that Wes Gray was following.

'Are you Mrs Trantor?' he asked. 'The sheriff said I might get a room here.'

'Of course. There's one ready for you. I was a bit concerned that you might ride on when you heard that your friend was dead. Or take a room at the saloon.'

Wes Gray was surprised by the young woman's words. 'You talk like you were expecting me,' he said, 'perhaps you've mistaken me for someone else.'

'No,' she told him, 'I know who you are. Even if your fight with Carter and Oates hadn't become the topic on everyone's lips I would have known you from my father's description. You're Wes Gray, sometimes known as Medicine Feather. My father sometimes used your Sioux name Wiyaka Wakan. But whatever name you choose to go by, my father never doubted that you would come.'

'Your father?'

'John Philip Trantor. I don't know how he came by the name Crackaway. Perhaps you can tell me.'

Wes Gray shook his head, not only to deny any knowledge of the derivation of Crackaway but mainly because he'd known the man for more than twenty years and had never heard him speak of any family. He removed his hat and held it by the brim while he

34

observed the girl.

'I'm Jenny,' she told him. 'Mother and I moved here from Ohio two years ago.' She expanded the family story, telling Wes how her father had gone in search of gold when she was a baby and when that failed to bring in the riches he required he had turned his hand to hunting and trapping. That period in his life, as Wes knew from his own experiences, had proved to be no more profitable; fashion and excessive hunting had combined to put an end to the once lucrative trade in beaver pelts. Crackaway had barely managed to scrape together enough money to support himself and his family from one year to the next. Then the war had erupted and his services as a scout had become invaluable to the Union cause, but still failed to fill the coffers of the Trantor family and at the end of hostilities had headed west once more, hunting meat for the railroad gangs and scouting for the army in their Indian campaigns. Eventually, when he'd amassed sufficient money to purchase a strip of land he could settle on and farm, he'd sent for his wife and daughter and they'd arranged to meet up in this frontier town before heading west to the site he'd selected near Colorado Springs. Before he could join them, however, the army pressed him into service once again. The Black Hills campaign in the summer of 1876 had effectively ended the military resistance of the Plains Indians, but small bands remained at large in defiance of the government's policies. It took more than a year to wheedle them all out of the hills and on to reservations. By early 1878 only Sitting Bull commanded a tribe that roamed free but they had crossed the border into Canada. Crackaway's usefulness to the army was at an end.

'Sadly,' Jenny told Wes Gray, 'my mother died before being reunited with Dad. He's buried near to her.'

The question uppermost in Wes Gray's mind concerned the name on his old friend's marker. Although he had always known him as Crackaway, it seemed strange that his proper name had not been used by his daughter.

'He didn't want anyone to know I was his daughter,' Jenny told him. 'He was protecting me.'

'From what?'

'Something that he'd discovered on his journey here. Something that it was dangerous to know.'

'What was it?' pressed Wes.

'I'm not sure. He was still gathering information when he was killed.'

'The sheriff told me his body was found trampled in the stable. General opinion has it that he was sleeping off a drinking session. Do you agree?'

'Of course not. Pretending to be drunk was his excuse for hanging around the saloon where he hoped to pick up the information he was seeking. People assumed he was permanently drunk because he threw whiskey on his shirt so that the smell of alcohol accompanied him wherever he went.'

Wes Gray was content to accept the girl's explanation, it was more in keeping with the man he'd known than the notion of a town drunk. It still didn't explain why he was in the stable or how he'd met his death under the feet of the animals. Accidents happened to the most experienced horsemen and perhaps Crackaway had just been in the wrong place at the wrong time, but Jenny's story had tilted his thinking towards murder. 'Don't you have any clue about what your father had become involved in or why he sent for me?'

'I only know that he'd sent a message to you before he arrived in town. He wanted me to go with you to Council Bluffs, to wait there for him until he'd done what needed to be done here.'

'But you don't know what that was.'

'It might have had something to do with John Lord. Dad didn't like him coming here or pestering me, but I'm sure he was wary of him before he was aware that he was a nuisance to me.'

'John Lord appears to be an important man in this town.'

'He is. He has a large spread south of here and also owns a lot of properties in town. He either owns or holds the deeds to the premises of most of the businesses in Palmersville and has no hesitation in using his power to get his own way. Everything he does is to advance his own wealth and power. He's ruthless and I believe merciless to anyone he sees as a stumbling block to his ambition.'

Wes had known such men in the past and expected to meet more in the future. They weren't a rare breed in any part of the world, but that provided no specific indication to the purpose of Crackaway's crusade. Wes looked at the daughter; her green eyes were fixed intently on his face. When he asked if she thought John Lord was responsible for her father's death they darkened slightly then narrowed as she considered her reply. It was clear that she wanted to say yes but also obvious that she had no grounds for making such a claim.

'They argued,' she told Wes. 'It was the night my father died. John Lord came here to persuade me to marry him. My father was in the room, pretending to be drunk and asleep and doggedly refused to go when John Lord tried to chase him away. There was a scuffle, which ended with John Lord on the floor and his gun in my father's hand. I told him to leave, which he did, but the menace in the expression he threw at Father could easily have been a death sentence.'

Jenny's account seemed to point to the fact that if John Lord had killed Crackaway it was due to being bested in front of a woman he was trying to impress and not because of the quest embarked upon by the old man.

'And your father died that night?'

'Yes.'

There was something in the poise of her body, the angle at which she held her head that suggested to Wes that the girl expected him to announce a plan of revenge; that she believed that he would exact vengeance for Crackaway's death. Initially, such a thought barely existed for him but he knew it was there, flitting through his psyche without substance, an uncatchable butterfly that showed its wings for an instant before disappearing into the back reaches of his mind; Crackaway had been a friend and if his death had not been an accident then someone had to seek justice for him. It wasn't right to let the task fall to the girl who was his only family, and the sheriff had already decided that no crime had been committed by permitting the immediate burial of the body. So by default it was his duty to uncover the truth of the matter.

But even if he couldn't find proof that Crackaway's death had been other than an accident he was unwilling to leave Palmersville without unearthing the reason for his summons. Crackaway's daughter believed he'd been brought to town merely to escort her to Council Bluffs but, if so, then Crackaway's reason for remaining in Palmersville must have been of some importance. He'd spent a lifetime struggling to amass the wherewithal to provide her with a decent home so it was only natural to assume he would want to go with her. Wes was determined to resolve the matter but he was short of information. Talking to Bob Best seemed to be the logical starting point.

It soon became apparent that Jenny Trantor had no other lodgers. Because of her impending removal from Palmersville she had been reluctant to take in any new paying guests, but the townsfolk, in ignorance of her plans to leave town, attributed her empty rooms to the recent death of her mother. One person, however, did arrive to take an evening meal with them. Harry Portlass was a lawyer with a small office on the block down the street from the bank. He was a tall, fair-haired man probably a decade younger than Wes, well-groomed and wearing a smart store-bought suit with brown, polished boots. When introduced, he was instantly wary of Wes Gray, as though in awe of his reputation and anticipating some violent or uncivilized demonstration of his frontier lifestyle. But, as the minutes passed, it was clear that Harry Portlass's trepidation was in respect of the house owner's safety. It didn't escape Wes's notice that the lawyer's eyes followed every movement made by Jenny Trantor, desperate for a glance or a smile to be cast in his direction. As a consequence, when the meal was finished, Wes left the couple alone, at first stepping outside to drink his coffee then following the narrow lane that led back to the main street.

At the end of the street a lantern burned brightly on a pole outside the forge but the doors were closed and Wes figured that the blacksmith had finished his business for the day. He was hoping to speak with Bob Best and the only possibility for doing so this night was if he found him in the saloon. Even if he hadn't become acquainted with it earlier in the day he would have found it the easiest place in town to find. Not only were there coal-oil lamps burning all along its frontage, but the silhouettes of customers showed clearly against the building's big glass windows. There was noise, too; a mumbling, grumbling sound that rose to a crescendo when Wes pushed aside the batwing doors to gain admittance to one of the smallest barrooms he'd ever been in.

The place was full, not only of men but more

especially noise. The hubbub reminded him of the crash of the waterfalls and white water stretches of the upper Missouri where the river's impenetrable noise belittled man's voice. But this noise consisted solely of the voices of men, a hundred conversations being conducted at full volume. It was an atmosphere that Wes didn't enjoy, but this was the only saloon in town and he had nowhere else to go. He pushed his way through the throng to join the crush of people ranged along the bar.

Bob Best wasn't difficult to spot in the crowded room. Even though he was half stooped against the counter he seemed to cause a ripple effect among the men lining the bar every time he shifted his shoulders to lift his glass to his lips. He raised his head slightly when his eyes focused on the buckskin-clad figured farther along the counter. Bob spoke a few words to his companion, adding a head movement to direct the other's attention towards Wes, then pushed himself upright when he saw the frontiersman, beer glass in hand, heading towards him.

'I wanted a word,' Wes told the blacksmith when he reached him, 'but it's a bit loud in here for conversation.'

Bob Best laughed. 'It's the penalty we're paying for having a celebrity in town.'

'Who is that?'

'You, Mr Gray. Everyone's heard your name. You're as famous as Davy Crockett, Kit Carson and Wild Bill Hickock.'

The blacksmith's words didn't bring Wes any

41

pleasure. In his opinion, his only claim to fame was the fact that he had survived those forces of nature which had taken the lives of many others, but he couldn't take any credit for that. In the main it had been due to the generosity and protection of the various tribes with whom he'd travelled and wintered. They had taught him how to live off the land, had sheltered him when homeless and cured him when ill. Whenever he tried to explain those facts to his fellow Americans, his words were brushed aside like autumn leaves. Now he didn't try but nor did he try to claim unearned glory. 'You know who I am!'

'Sheriff Johnson was quick to spread the word.'

'Why did he do that?'

'Perhaps, like me, he hopes you're in town to stay.'

'Why would he want that?'

Bob Best turned his head a little to the side, directed his gaze to one of the tables around which a group of men were gambling over the cards in their hands. Among them were Carter and Oates. Both men were studiously avoiding making eye contact with the men at the bar, but it was equally obvious that both were aware of Wes Gray's presence. 'I guess the sheriff was as impressed with the way you turned the tables on those two in here as I was with the way you handled John Lord and his hirelings outside the cemetery. One man has too much power in this town. If the community is going to develop then changes need to be made.'

'And you think I'm the man to do that?'

'Certainly.'

42

'Sorry to disappoint you but you're wrong.'

'We're not expecting you to do it without reward. Hal here,' Bob Best indicated his companion, 'is a leading figure on the town committee and he's sure that they'll pay well to be rid of John Lord and his cronies. Their grip on the town is suffocating trade and development.'

Wes Gray held up a hand to put an end to the blacksmith's oratory. When he spoke he could barely conceal the anger from his voice. 'I don't know what help you think I can be. I'm not a hired gun.'

'No, no,' Bob Best replied, 'I didn't mean to imply anything of that sort, but you stood up to John Lord. He is as much in awe of your reputation as any other man in this town. You've neutralized his power and if that continues the tradespeople and the citizens have more hope of thriving.' He looked to his companion for assistance. 'This is Hal Adamson. He runs the mercantile store. Tell him, Hal. Tell him that the town will go under if we don't rid ourselves of the shackles that Lord has put on us.'

In appearance, Hal Adamson was the polar opposite of the blacksmith. He was a short man with a grocer's paunch, had thin, flattened black hair and a large moustache. He wore a wool jacket, below which a watch chain stretched across his body in a double swag from one waistcoat pocket to another. 'We do need help,' he said.

Wes shook his head. 'I'll be leaving soon. I came here to meet my friend, Crackaway. He's dead and I have no other reason to stay. But I did want to ask

43

you,' he turned his attention back to Bob Best, 'about his death.'

'I don't think there's anything I can tell you.'

'I'm told his body was discovered in the livery stable. Did you find him?'

'Yes. I don't know what he was doing there. General opinion is that he was sleeping off another heavy session. He certainly liked liquor. Whenever I came in here he was slumped across a table with a bottle in his hand.'

'Had he slept in your stable at any other time?'

'No. Not to my knowledge. Came along to check on his horse a couple of times and pay for his feed.'

'Was he sober then?'

'Sober enough.'

'What kind of animal is the horse that stamped on him?'

'Placid most of the time. The old man must have done something drastic to startle her like that.'

'You're sure it was the horse that killed him?'

'Yes. She was still skittish when I got into her stall and there were blood spatters on her fetlocks and chest.'

There was nothing in the blacksmith's story that differed from what the sheriff had told him, nothing that hinted at anything other than the accident that people seemed to think were the just desserts of a town drunk. But Wes knew that Crackaway had been playing a role; he wasn't a drunk and he had no need to find a bed in a stable. So what had led him to his brutal death? Perhaps he wouldn't find the answer in

Palmersville. There was only one other person who might be able to help but to find him meant retracing his steps for twenty miles. 'I'll need my horse at first light,' he told Bob Best then finished his drink and returned to Jenny Trantor's boarding house.

FOUR

When he'd woken that morning at the foot of the high, tree-lined ridge on the west bank of the Missouri, Wes Gray had lit a small fire to make coffee. The chill from the winter snow which still clung to the northern high ground had carried down the valley with determination and it was clear that the new day's sun would need to gather a lot more strength before it could begin to warm the ground. This camp site, secluded behind a spit of land that jutted into the great river, was one of Wes's regular haunts. He'd pulled his canoe ashore at this point every year as he made his annual springtime journey east from the village of his Arapaho wife's tribe on the Snake River. For ten years he had rendezvoused at Council Bluffs with his old friend Caleb Dodge and together they had led settlers halfway across the continent to the territories along the Pacific coast. That morning, as he watched the growing orange glow of morning light and listened to the sounds of the awakening day, he had wondered how many more such journeys there would be. The day of the covered wagon was almost over. Railways were able to carry people west in a fraction of the time and with the minimum of discomfort. In addition, on his last visit to California, he'd read a newspaper article which trumpeted the determination of some French engineers to construct a canal in Panama which would make sea travel a viable route from the east coast to western seaports.

As he chewed pemmican and warmed his hands on his coffee-filled tin mug, these thoughts passed through his mind but they didn't prevent him hearing the rustle caused by movement among the trees behind him. He didn't move. He was on a stretch of the river that marked the boundary of the territory that was designated as the Great Sioux Reservation by the Laramie Treaty in 1868 and, although the government had recently reneged on that agreement to give the gold hunters that vital strip in the Black Hills, this area was still out of bounds to most Americans. But Wes Gray was not most Americans. He was Wiyaka Wakan, Medicine Feather, brother of the Arapaho and friend of the Sioux on whose behalf he had spoken at councils and treaty meetings with the Americans. In addition to his Arapaho wife in the western lands, he also had a Sioux wife, Apo Hopa, who lived on their farm on a 'V' of land where the Mildwater Creek met the South Platte River.

Wes knew that whoever had him under observation wanted him to know they were close, that they were approaching his camp with friendly intentions. He continued chewing the pemmican until he was sure his visitor had broken away from the cover of the trees then turned his head to look over his shoulder.

There was only one man, not a young warrior nor yet an ancient, too old to fight in battle. He was Ogallalah Sioux, a brave far from his traditional territory. He wore leggings and a cotton shirt and his hair was braided in two plaits that reached to his chest each side of his neck. Two eagle feathers were attached to the back of his head by an ornament of buffalo bone. Only a blanket of dried grass separated him from the horse he sat astride. It was black, it's colour fading to dapple on its hindquarters. The ropes from which the bridle and reins had been created were also made from plaited grasses. Feathers were tied to the ropes and also into the horse's mane. In his left hand the man held on to a leather strap that was attached to a second horse, a long-backed pinto which was harnessed with an American bridle and saddle.

Wes stretched out the hand that held the tin cup, an invitation for the Indian to step down and join him at the small fire.

When he'd drunk some of the hot liquid, the Ogallalah told Wes that his name was Wapaha Sapa, Black Lance. Wes wondered what had brought Black Lance so far east but such were the times that the aftermath of the Black Hills War had forced many of those Ogallalah, Hunkpapa and Minneconjou who had battled the Bluecoats at the Rosebud, Little Bighorn and Slim Buttes to find shelter among their less war-like Santee and Blackfoot cousins. It was often difficult to penetrate the stoic expression on a Sioux brave's face and that of Black Lance was no different, but although he held his head high he could not hide from Wes the dull-eyed gaze of a hunted man.

Crackaway had chosen Black Lance as his message carrier because he had learned that he was the uncle of Apo Hopa, Wes's Sioux wife. Along with the call for help, the Ogallalah had brought a good pony to carry Medicine Feather to the town which was many miles from the river. In addition, he promised to protect Wes's possessions until he returned. Although eager to reach Council Bluffs, Wes was aware that Caleb Dodge wouldn't yet be ready to order the wagons west. Plenty of time remained for him to complete his journey. Besides, a message from Crackaway was, in itself, an intimation of importance and urgency, so Wes lost no time in finding a suitable place to cross the river and make tracks south-easterly to Palmersville.

The discussion with Bob Best hadn't added anything to Wes's knowledge of his old friend's demise. There were no known witnesses to his death and, with the exception of his daughter, no one in Palmersville was interested enough to investigate Crackaway's presence in the stable. His portrayal of a town drunk had been good enough to convince everyone. The assumption that he'd stumbled into the stable to sleep off a gut full of whiskey had been accepted without question, except by Wes. Whatever his friend had been up to he had been anxious not to have his daughter involved. For her safety he had even refused to acknowledge her, and had sent for Wes to take her to Council Bluffs. The implication was that Crackaway knew that the consequences he faced if his activities were discovered would be drastic. If they had cost Crackaway his life then Wes wanted to know the reason why. He had no more clues to follow in town but perhaps Black Lance could supply some answers.

When they'd met on the banks of the Missouri, the Ogallalah Sioux had spoken little, informing Wes only that he had been watching for him for many days. He had told Wes where to find Crackaway but not why he needed to see him. Perhaps Black Lance didn't know anything, had been nothing more than a messenger, but Wes knew no one else who might be a source of information.

Jenny Trantor was alone when he returned to his lodging. The announcement that he was leaving Palmersville early next morning took her by surprise.

'I can't leave tomorrow,' she told him, 'that's too soon. There are arrangements to make for this house and furniture. I need a few days. Besides,' she added, her tone laced with disappointment, 'I hoped you would investigate my father's death, try to find out what he was hoping to uncover.'

'I am trying,' Wes told her, 'but I'm not sure that anyone in this town can help me. I'm going in search of the man who passed on your father's message. Perhaps he can help me.' For a moment he studied Jenny Trantor. Eventually he asked if she was sure she had told him everything she knew.

'There was one thing,' she told him and asked him to wait while she went to one of the upstairs rooms. 'He came in with this one night,' she declared and handed over an empty sack that had been used for vegetables or grain. 'He seemed to attach some importance to it, kept looking at the marking on the bottom.'

Wes Gray had already seen the US Government brand in an unusual red design.

'Why would Dad be interested in an old sack?' Jenny asked.

Wes Gray didn't have an answer for her but he asked if he could keep it. He would take it with him when he rode out in the morning.

Bob Best parted company with Hal Adamson at the saloon doors. Bob went left, up the street to the stable and a final check on the stock before heading for his bed in the adjoining house. There was seldom any urgency for an early start to the day but Wes Gray had ordered his pinto fed and ready for travel at first light. Although, in the main, the frontiersman's manner had been quiet and inoffensive, his reputation was that of a man it was best not to rile; if he wanted his horse at first light then Bob would have it saddled and ready when he got to the door.

Hal Adamson had a shorter walk home. His emporium was one block down from the saloon at the other side of the street. It wasn't until he'd put his key in the lock that he realized that someone was standing in the darkest corner of his covered boardwalk. 'Who's there?' he asked.

The figure pushed himself away from the wall and took three or four paces forward. Even before he was close enough to be recognizable in the dim light, the store-owner had identified Clem Oates by his ungainly shuffle. Despite the night-time chill, Clem Oates wore no coat and his sleeves were rolled up high on his thick arms. His thumbs were hooked into the front of his gunbelt in menacing fashion.

Hal Adamson took a step back, a gesture which expressed his reluctance to open up his premises in the presence of Clem Oates more eloquently than words could have done. 'What do you want?' he asked, but before he'd completed the short question hands gripped his shoulders from behind and dragged him off the boardwalk into the side alley.

'You're keeping bad company, storekeeper,' Tad Carter hissed at him as he thrust him against the wall.

'What do you mean?' Hal Adamson couldn't keep the nervousness out of his voice.

'I mean the Injun lover. You and him were talking like old pals.'

Hal Adamson shook his head in denial. 'It was Bob Best he wanted to speak to.'

'What about?'

Hal Adamson was a founder member of the town committee with good intentions for the betterment of the community but his physical bravery rarely matched up to his civic ambitions. Even though he believed in law and order and wanted to oppose the tyranny of people like John Lord and the violence of men like Carter and Oates, he was afraid of them. For a moment he paused before answering, a mental struggle prohibiting him from amassing the necessary words.

Clem Oates prompted the storekeeper by driving a large fist into his midriff. Hal Adamson gasped, his knees buckled but he was prevented from falling by the rough grip that Tad Carter had on his coat. He was hauled upright and thrust against the wall. Oates and Carter cast glances towards the main street to make sure that they weren't being observed.

Carter repeated his question. 'What were you talking about?'

'He was asking questions about the old man that was killed.' Hal wanted to double over, relieve the pain in his stomach, but Carter held on to him, forced his shoulders against the wall and stared menacingly into his eyes.

'What questions?'

'Questions about how he'd died. Seems he came to Palmersville to meet him. They were friends.'

Angrily, Oates shifted the grip he had on Hal Adamson so that he held him by the lapels of his jacket and could more easily shake his victim and bounce his head off the wall behind. 'What did you tell him?'

'Nothing. Bob Best did the talking. He found the body and it was his horse that killed the old man. He told Wes Gray it had been an accident.'

'And he believed him?'

'Why shouldn't he? That's what everyone else believes.'

Clem Oates released his hold on the storekeeper and allowed him to straighten his clothing. Tad Carter pushed himself between, demanding to know what else Hal Adamson had learned about the frontiersman's visit.

'Only that it's over. He's quitting town early in the morning. He told Bob Best to have his horse ready at first light.'

That was a snippet that Carter felt sure would be of interest to John Lord. He signalled with his head for Clem to get their horses while he gave a last bit of advice to Hal Adamson.

'Remember, Mr Lord doesn't like his people to shoot off their mouth to strangers. We'll be watching you, storekeeper, so don't step out of line.'

'I'm not one of Mr Lord's people,' Hal insisted, trying desperately to infuse this show of resistance with determination.

Without hesitation, Tad Carter sank his fist with tremendous force into Hal's stomach and with the air driven from his body the storekeeper sank to his knees. His assailant leant forward and hissed words over his head that shackled him as surely as chains in a prison cell. 'Yes, you are and don't ever forget it.'

John Lord had spent the evening poring over his stock books, ledgers and correspondence, calculating current assets and future profits. When he'd finished with them he poured a good measure of whiskey into a tumbler as a suitable token of his growing wealth. He swallowed a mouthful. It was good but failed to relax the stern expression that had been on his face all night. His growing wealth was a source of satisfaction but he'd had plans to make this night significant for other reasons.

He'd wanted Jenny Trantor from the first moment he'd seen her. Without exception she was the most eligible woman in the territory to be his permanent companion. He'd even been prepared to offer her marriage and a home built and furnished to her own style. Her refusal to accept his overtures had, at first, amused him as some feminine game to tantalize him while secretly intending to accept when she'd toyed with him long enough. After all, as he repeated to himself on frequent occasions, who else in this barely civilized country could offer her an existence with even half the luxury that he was able to provide? No, eventually she would succumb. But it had been almost a year since she had first refused his advances and recently her resistance had become more determined and marked with annoyance. Consequently, his addresses to her had been laced with more aggression. No matter what her reasons were, he was not to be rejected. He had decided that he was going to possess her and he never failed to get what he wanted.

If her lodger, Crackaway, had not interfered a few nights earlier then he would have succeeded, but that old man couldn't get between them again. His anger rose when he remembered how she'd openly spurned him earlier that day, had embarrassed him in front of his hired hands. It was an insult she would have to pay for. She had refused him for the last time.

First though he had to wait for Wes Gray to leave town. The man that some folk called Medicine Feather had declared himself her protector and if the rumours about him were to be believed he was not a man to oppose. Tad Carter had made that discovery before the frontiersman had been in town an hour. John Lord decided it was necessary to wait a while longer but as soon as Wes Gray quit town Jenny Trantor would be his. Those thoughts filled his head when he heard the horses gallop into the compound.

In the main, the news brought by Carter and Oates lifted John Lord's spirits. Wes Gray's departure from Palmersville was, at that moment, his fondest desire. The information that the frontiersman was Crackaway's friend was less palatable.

'You're sure he doesn't suspect anything.'

'I'm not sure of anything,' Carter replied. 'I'm just repeating what Hal Adamson told us.'

'Well let's not take any chances,' John Lord announced after a moment's thought. 'If he's leaving town tomorrow let's make sure he never comes back.'

Tad Carter grinned. 'That's what I was hoping you'd say, boss. I'll tail him out of town and leave him somewhere along the trail. Wherever he's going he won't get there.'

'That's the right idea,' said Lord, 'but it's a job for Oates.' He turned to the other man and told him to pick a couple of hands to ride with him. 'Gray will be a lot more trouble than that old man if he ever finds out what we're doing, so make sure he doesn't survive.'

Tad Carter wasn't pleased. He was the one who had been pinned down by Wes Gray, the one humiliated by having the point of the frontiersman's knife prick his throat, so the task of putting a bullet in his head should be his honour. John Lord, however, had other duties for the surly cowboy.

'I've had word that the next shipment will be arriving in Spearpoint tomorrow. You need to get the crew organized. Move that infected herd out to Blain's Canyon and Oates, after you've settled with Wes Gray, you can meet up with them to help with the Missouri crossing.'

FIVE

They were little more than a mile out of Palmersville and pale, long shadows were just beginning to stretch ahead as they headed west in the new day's light. The horse had its neck stretched low and forward in that careful way, giving the impression it had been woken too early and was too weary to be on the road at this early hour. It was an idiosyncrasy that didn't fool its rider who could feel the power of the animal and figured it could run all day if he required it to do so. They had been travelling at a steady pace, following the recognized trail, the one which had brought them to town and which later would veer south towards Spearpoint and onwards to Council Bluffs, Independence and Kansas City.

Suddenly, the pinto's ears pricked up, alerted by a sound or a smell that had carried on the breeze. It raised its head, turning it to the left as though seeking the cause of its interest. It's rider, Medicine Feather, noted its behaviour but could detect no hint of fear or alarm. The animal hadn't shied or rolled its eyes in the nervous manner of horses when a grizzly or wolf was in the vicinity; perhaps it had caught the scent of a pronghorn or another horse. He rubbed its neck then reined in and dismounted.

While he adjusted the saddle straps, Wes Gray took the opportunity to scan the surrounding country. To the left, a timbered escarpment rose, a densely wooded hillside that dropped away on the far side to fallow land where a few small farms had been established. On the other side of the trail the ground was less sumptuous, tending towards the terrain more usual in the north country, rocky and boulder strewn. That was where the silver had been discovered that had pumped a little life into Palmersville. He was about to remount when a team of six pulling a high-sided wagon hove into view on the trail ahead. Its rattling, he figured, could have been the cause of the pinto's curiosity. Climbing into the saddle, he waited at the side of the trail until the vehicle had passed by.

At first, it seemed that the wagon would rumble on its way to Palmersville without anything more than a cursory salutation from the two people on the high-board, but two lengths beyond the horseman, the driver hauled his team to a halt. Standing, so that he could see over the high side of the wagon, the driver called to the frontiersman.

'Wes Gray?'

Wes nudged the pinto into motion until he reached the front of the wagon.

The driver was a man in his forties with facial hair

that rested on his chest. On his head was an old, sweat-stained, high-crowned felt hat and he wore cross-belted bibbed-overalls and a rough wool, linen-coloured shirt. His eyes were small and dark but the expression on his face was not unpleasant. 'I was bringing my sister into town to see you. Says the pair of you are acquainted.'

Wes glanced at the second person on the high-board. She was several years younger than her brother and dressed in bonnet and shawl in the manner common with women across the frontier. 'Mr Gray,' she said, 'it's some time since we last saw each other.'

Wes Gray removed his hat when he recognized Kitty Belton. He had first known her as Calico Kit working in a now extinct railhead town east of Cheyenne. She had taken his dollar on more than one occasion, just as she'd taken the dollar of Joe Belton the soldier she'd later married. Kitty wasn't the only saloon girl he'd known who had got out of that business by marrying a customer, but he'd also known others who had taken up that life to escape the loneliness and drudgery entailed in being a settler's wife. He was critical of none. Even though the freedom of frontier life was idyllic for him, he was aware of its hardships. Everyone had to find their own method of survival.

Wes had last seen Kitty and Joe four years ago at Fort Supply. Their plan then had been to buy a farm when Joe's time with the army was completed. Wes's supposition that they had found a suitable site around Palmersville was short lived.

'Did you not hear?' Kitty said. 'Joe was transferred to the Seventh Cavalry at the wrong time. He was due to be discharged in the fall. He didn't deserve to be at the Little Bighorn when Custer's luck ran out.'

In Wes's opinion no one deserved to be at the Greasy Grass site that day, and he had his own view on Custer's luck but he kept it to himself. 'You're up and about early,' he observed.

'I've got a load of freight to collect,' Kitty's brother, Rafe Leeward, told him. 'Kitty hoped to see you before you left town.'

'We nearly missed you,' his sister laughed, 'in more ways than one. We were so busy watching those riders on the hillside that we almost didn't see you.'

Instinctively, Wes raised his eyes to the tree-lined slopes. He couldn't see any riders, hadn't seen any riders but perhaps they were the reason for the pinto's reaction and not the more obvious approaching wagon.

'I thought they were Mr Lord's men,' Rafe explained, 'but they normally ride out to Spearpoint with the wagons.'

'You work for John Lord?' Wes asked.

'Contracted to haul freight for him. Bring goods from the Spearpoint railhead and then transport them to the Sioux Agency on the Cheyenne River.'

'Why do you bring the goods to Palmersville? Why don't you take the load directly to the Agency?'

'We store them in Mr Lord's warehouse until the cattle arrive then we all travel together to deter robbers. The goods are valuable.'

61

'How many wagons make the trip?'

'Ten. Sometimes a dozen. Not all as big as this one, but there's a substantial load of food and goods every time.' Rafe Leeward had a rueful expression. 'Got to make as many trips as I can. The railway spur's been built up to Spearpoint and when the engineers get a bridge across the Missouri it'll be the death of my business.'

Wes could sympathize with the man; he'd entertained similar thoughts regarding his own life recently. It wasn't only the Indians who were suffering from the pace of American expansion. No one had expected such an overwhelming determination to settle the territories beyond the Missouri, nor the new technology to achieve it. He told Kitty that he intended to return to Palmersville and promised to visit her before leaving for Council Bluffs. Then he pressed his heels to the pinto's flanks and continued on the trail west.

As soon as he was out of sight of the wagon he halted again, stepping down and lifting the pinto's rear leg as if inspecting the shoe for a trapped stone. In fact he was troubled by the information that there were riders on the hillside so, from behind the horse's hindquarters, he scanned the trees for a sign that the men were still up there. Common sense told him that it was nothing more than coincidence; there was no reason why other people shouldn't be abroad so early in the day and there was no good reason to suppose they were interested in him, but the suggestion that they were John Lord's men had sown a seed of caution. Bob Best had implied that Carter and Oates wouldn't be fussy how they achieved their revenge for the saloon fight so an ambush was a real possibility, and he'd made an enemy of John Lord, too, by promoting himself as Jenny Trantor's protector.

Although the movements were slight, a horse tossing its head, the swish of a tail that disturbed a bush, they were enough to inform him that whoever was in the hills had him under observation. There was a flash of steel as the rising sun glinted on a bridle buckle or ornamentation, and then the snort of an impatient horse, which only reached Wes because his senses were keen to pick up the smallest warning sign. The pinto shook its head to indicate that it had heard the noise too. Wes put down its foot and climbed into the saddle. He figured they were probably still too close to Palmersville for an ambush to be attempted along this stretch of the trail. He'd already encountered Rafe Leeward and his sister so there was a possibility of other people heading to or from town. If murder was on their minds they would want a much more isolated spot. Wes chose to oblige them.

Unhurriedly, he followed the trail for a couple of hundred yards then veered away to his right, towards the rockier high country to the north. He'd chosen to leave the trail at the point where a huge boulder obscured him from the watchers to the south. If they were hunting him they would have to quit the cover of the trees and expose themselves to his gun.

This was new terrain for him, territory he'd never before travelled, but he had total belief in his ability to outwit his pursuers. He entered a long winding passage, a dry, narrow valley that descended from the trail before rising to the far high ground. It was populated by a few trees that became more sparse on the distant heights. The undulations and twists of the valley were an advantage, providing many stretches where he would be hidden from the sight of pursuers. In addition, there were many offshoots, gulches and ravines from which a man could spring his own ambush.

The first task, however, was to ensure that he was indeed the prey of the men on the hillside. He halted his horse under a spring-dressed coyote willow, stood on the saddle and reached up to grab one of the lower, sturdy branches. He hauled himself upward and then climbed until he had a view to the far side of the trail. He counted three riders, each finding his own path down the hillside, leaning back in the saddle to distribute their weight to their mount's advantage. There was a hint of recklessness to their riding, a reflection of their need to keep on Wes's trail. From his observation point he had no doubt that they were after him.

Back in the saddle, he urged his horse forward, demanding from it the speed he had always felt it capable of producing. Half a mile ahead there were draws to left and right, if he could reach them before his pursuers entered the valley then he would double the advantage he had over them. At present, they had no reason to suspect that their presence was known to him, and it was probable that they would split up if they had to find him again. He threw a look back down the trail as he turned the pinto into the gully on his right. No one had entered the valley.

It was a blind draw, but deep enough and with walls irregular enough to provide cover and hiding places. Anyone searching for him would have to ride its full length. Towards its farthest point an angled niche offered itself as a suitable place to tether the pinto. He took his rope and scaled the face of the wall that would give him a view into the main valley. It took him a few minutes but in fact he had no need to hurry.

His hunters had made slow progress and were at that moment grouped in discussion not far beyond the tree he had used earlier as a lookout post. Wes watched them with satisfaction; they were behaving as he had predicted. Because they hadn't been able to see him on the trail ahead they had been forced to assume he'd ridden along one of the offshoots but the ground was too hard to see the prints of the horse's hoofs and if they were determined to capture him, each one would require investigation. From forty feet above, Wes Gray observed the trio. The centre man whom he identified as Clem Oates, was directing the other two, ordering one down the gully to the left and the other to the right where the pinto grazed in its secluded coomb. Oates, with his rifle upright on his thigh, advanced slowly, ready to add his firepower to that of the outrider who flushed Wes Gray into the open.

Wes scurried back down the hillside. He had already chosen the manner of his first victim's death and needed to be in position before the unfortunate man came across the pinto. To reach the spot where the horse was tethered it would be necessary for his stalker to pass under a thick cottonwood. Wes would be waiting. If these men were prepared to ambush him, show no mercy, then they had to expect the same treatment. He was in the tree, lying motionless in a forked branch when he heard the slow clop of a walking horse approaching. The pinto stretched its neck forward, keeping its head low like a penitent in church as though aware that violence and death were close at hand.

The man carried his rifle across his body, the weapon was cocked and his finger was inside the trigger guard. His approach was cautious but he meant to shoot first. He would kill Medicine Feather mercilessly. There would be no explanation for the deed. Someone wanted the scout dead and this man was prepared to see it done. He was a short man with a small moustache and bristles on his jaw. There was a moment when it seemed that he was satisfied that his quarry had not ventured into this draw, that he would abandon his search and rejoin his companions, but for thoroughness he nudged his animal on another few steps and was directly below the tree when he saw the pinto. Instantly he swung his rifle, certain that Wes, too, would be within that niche with the animal. Wes Gray dropped the noose around his neck and pulled with every ounce of strength.

The man was lifted from his saddle, the rifle fell from his hands and his legs kicked wildly, striking his horse and startling it so that it jumped forward to leave him swinging on the end of the rope.

Frantically, he grabbed at the rope around his throat, desperate to relieve its tightening hold. In the grip of fear and pain he twisted in the air, unable to make a sound, unable to do anything to get air into his lungs or to stop his descent into unconsciousness and the onset of death.

When the man was dead, Wes let go of the rope which, prior to the man's arrival, he had secured to another branch. The man hung ugly from the tree but it evoked no pity in his slayer. Wes Gray hadn't survived in a world of kill or be killed by acts of mercy. When it was necessary to kill a man it didn't much matter how it was done. He picked up the rifle and fired a shot in the air. This, he suspected, would bring Clem Oates in a hurry, believing that his companion had either found Wes's trail or had already killed him. He took a position behind a rock, withdrew his hunting knife and waited.

To his surprise it wasn't Clem Oates who came galloping along the valley, it was the third man. The draw he'd been sent to investigate had been a lot smaller than this one. It was probable that Oates was close behind. Wes watched and waited.

As he came around the bluff and into full view of the tree from which the other man's body dangled in grotesque fashion, the man hauled on the reins. The shock of finding his friend's body affected him exactly as Wes had intended. The horse slithered forward on its haunches in its eagerness to obey the rider's command. The rider stared with disbelieving eyes at the blackening face of a companion with whom he'd shared breakfast less than an hour earlier. The realization that his own life was in jeopardy occurred to him a moment too late. He raised his rifle to fire a signal shot but the trigger was never pulled.

Even before the horse had come to a standstill, Wes Gray was on the move. With the stealth of a raiding Arapaho warrior he emerged from his hiding place and with two swift bounds silently covered the distance to his enemy. Vaulting on to the back of the horse so that he was behind the man, he squeezed his neck in the crook of his left arm while his right hand passed over the man's right shoulder and thrust the big knife deep into his heart. The blow killed him instantly with barely a sound uttered but his face wore a horrible grimace.

As Wes cast the body on the ground to lie under the dangling feet of the first man, a bullet whistled past his head and the crack of a rifle split the silence of the morning. Instinctively, Wes grabbed the reins, pressed himself low along the horse's neck and discarded his knife. He had his Colt in his hand just as a second shot, too, flew harmlessly past. He turned the horse and fired a shot at Clem Oates who was sighting along the barrel of his rifle once more. Wes's bullet flew close to Oates and his horse. The horse shied so that its rider's effort was even further wide of the mark than the previous two had been. He turned his own horse and set a course out of the draw and back to the valley. Wes gave chase, firing once more at his fleeing enemy.

No more shots were exchanged during the head-long gallop of the next few moments. Wes was gaining rapidly as they approached the mouth of the draw. He wanted to capture the last man, wanted to know if the attempt to kill had been ordered by John Lord or was in revenge for the beating that Carter had taken in the saloon fight. He fired a shot, deliberately over the other man's head in the hope that it would persuade him to stop. He didn't. Instead, he turned in the saddle and returned fire. It was a lucky shot. It hit the horse under Wes and it plunged, dying, on to the ground.

Wes rolled and came to his feet with his gun in his hand. Fifty yards away Chet Oates reined his mount to a halt and looked back. For a moment it seemed that he planned to charge Wes Gray but when he saw the scout still had his gun he changed his mind. He turned his horse and spurred it away from the draw and into the valley beyond.

Wes cursed. He was left with the task of killing the stricken animal that lay on the ground then walking back to where the pinto waited patiently. There was no point giving chase to Clem Oates, he would be miles away. They would meet again though, Wes was sure of that.

SIX

Although he stayed alert for any renewed attempt to ambush him, Wes saw no other sign of Clem Oates as he made his way to the Missouri then north to the place where he'd left his belongings. The meadowland of the river basin was lush and, when given the opportunity, the pinto proved he had a good appetite for a sustained run. They forded the river to the west bank and were reunited with Wapaha Sapa long before noon.

It was clear that Black Lance had been keeping watch for his return. He was waiting with folded arms by the upturned canoe in readiness to put it back in the water so that the scout could continue his journey downriver. But Wes wanted to palaver with the Indian so built a small fire and brewed a pot of coffee while they spoke. He imparted the news of Crackaway's death and his reluctance to believe it had been accidental. Then he questioned Black Lance about his meeting with Crackaway, eager to dig out what information he could about the reason for the message that had summoned him to Palmersville.

Like Wes, Crackaway was one of those men who had lived intermittently with tribes across the continent, and although they had sometimes fought side-by-side with the *wasicun*, the Americans, they had always shown such empathy for the plight of the Indians that their counsel was heeded even in the darkest moments of combat. For a year, Crackaway had been riding the Black Hills, seeking out those small bands of Sioux who were either reluctant or afraid to submit to the military, to persuade them that there was no future for them other than life on a reservation. It was a bitter message for an old trapper like Crackaway to deliver, but to put an end to the hardship and suffering that the resistance of the warriors inflicted on the women and children, he undertook it with the belief that he was doing the right thing.

He'd come east with the last of the bands, stopping at forts and soldier camps, following a route that would culminate in the rendezvous with his wife and daughter. The last leg of that journey had brought him through the territory of the Great Sioux Reservation. It was at the Indian Agency along the Cheyenne River that he had met Black Lance.

'Did something happen there?' Wes asked.

'When he saw the way we lived and were treated he became angry. It was not how he had told us it would be. The clothes and blankets we were promised are worn and without warmth. The cattle we are sent are thin and make our little ones sick. As it has always been, the *wasicun* are false. They speak of peace but

71

they only want the death of the Sioux, Cheyenne and all other tribes.'

Wes didn't want Black Lance's words to be true. He, too, had eventually added his voice to those of the peace commissioners in urging the tribes to lay down their weapons and live on reservations. In common with Crackaway, it was the desire to put an end to the deprivations conducive with a winter of being chivvied from one entrenchment to another that swayed his argument. His heart was with the warriors who wanted to continue to exist as their fathers and forefathers had done, but his brain told him that their military fight could never be won and the incessant pursuit was having a terrible affect on the women and children. But they had been promised fair treatment; he didn't want to believe that the words of the treaty makers had been nothing but hot air.

'Take me to the Agency,' Wes told Black Lance. 'Let me see what is happening there.'

The day had lost most of its light when Black Lance led the way into a settlement of a dozen tepees in a gulch through which ran water on its way to the Cheyenne River. The people were Ogallalah Sioux, Black Lance's kinsmen, who came out to greet his return and inspect his *wasicun* companion. There was none of the usual chatter and curiosity that had so often marked his arrival in villages. Instead, these people were silent, unusually morose for people whose natural, primitive emotion was to find laughter in all the aspects of adversity that the elements threw at them. But these people needed more than the recent arrival of spring to bring a semblance of comfort to their lives. They were battling more than the icy chill of winter. Food and substantial clothing would fill their bellies and keep their bodies warm but the persistent harrying and slaying of their warriors had finally destroyed their will to resist. They were starving, cold, frightened by their current situation and terrified of the future.

The leader of the group was a squat man, short in height but broad across the chest. His face, too, was squat with narrow eyes above a broad nose and mouth. Un-warrior-like, but matching Black Lance's attire, he wore a white-man's wool shirt above his leggings and had a grey blanket folded across his left shoulder as though it was a badge of office. He held a lance erect in his left hand, its butt rested on the ground. The feathers, ornaments and scalps attached to it fluttered in the wind. He registered no emotion as he faced Wes Gray but the men knew each other.

Pawnee Killer had lived in the village above the South Platte where Wes had first seen his wife, Apo Hopa. A few years earlier, Pawnee Killer, together with his friend Black Raven, had sought the death of Wes Gray in retribution for the murder of their sons, and although the true killers had later been identified and killed, their acrimony for the scout had never faded.

Wes raised his hand and uttered the greeting, '*Hau.*'

Empty of any pleasure at the white man's arrival, Pawnee Killer nonetheless observed the usual civility to a visitor, his right hand extending towards the mounted man then sweeping wide, an invitation to step down and share the fare that the women were preparing. It turned out to be as meagre as the appearance of the group predicted. He'd come at a bad time, Black Lance told him, because the promised rations were two weeks overdue and the rifles had been confiscated so they were unable to hunt for meat. The deprivation, Wes was assured, applied to every Sioux family registered at the Cheyenne River Agency.

Wes understood Crackaway's anger. This was not the life that had been promised to the Sioux; it was a betrayal, a humiliation that could only give birth to resentment and future rebellion. Perhaps, he thought, it was the government's plan to starve to death those Indians who hadn't been killed in battle.

Early next morning, accompanied by Black Lance, Wes shot a white-tailed deer drinking two miles upstream and returned to the small gathering with it slung over the Sioux's horse. It was repayment for the hospitality of the village but the prospect of fresh meat didn't generate rejoicing. As Black Lance predicted, the people were more concerned by the repercussions that might befall them if the gunshot had been heard by anyone at the Agency buildings. Pawnee Killer however, despite his personal animosity, accepted the gift, which would help to sustain his followers until the government shipment arrived.

The carcase had barely been claimed by the women who would gut and skin it and prepare it for the pot before two men rode rapidly into the encampment. They were Santee Sioux, each wearing a black Stetson and blue calico shirt with a red rag tied around the bicep of their left arm. They were also carrying rifles.

'Agency guards,' Black Lance muttered. 'The taller is Lame Dog and the other is Big Mouth.'

Lame Dog had ridden to the spot where the dead deer lay and inspected it while astride his pony. 'This animal has been shot,' he announced, 'who has a rifle?'

Wes stepped forward. 'I have.'

It was apparent to Wes that Lame Dog wanted to demonstrate his superiority over the people of this small village by announcing that the possession of firearms was against the rules of the Agency, but Wes was an American and not subject to the restrictions placed on those Ogallalah, Hunkpapa and other war-like nations who had submitted to the white man's terms.

'Who are you?' Lame Dog asked. 'What are you doing here? This land belongs to the Sioux.'

Wes chose to answer the last question first. 'I know that. My name is Wiyaka Wakan. My wife is Apo Hopa of the Ogallalah Sioux and I was invited here by her uncle.'

Black Lance moved so that he was standing shoulder to shoulder with Wes. 'I am Wapaha Sapa, the uncle of Apo Hopa. What this man says is true.'

Lame Dog wasn't appeased. 'You should have

reported to Mr Archer,' he told Wes. 'It is his responsibility to know who is living within the borders of the Agency.'

'I'm not living here,' Wes told him, 'just visiting, but I guess it would be polite to introduce myself to the Agent. I'll drop by his office later.'

Lame Dog and Big Mouth remained motionless for a few moments, unsure what action, if any, they should take against the American. Eventually, Lame Dog pointed at the dead animal and spoke in his native Santee tongue to two of the nearby Ogallalah warriors. When Wes asked for an interpretation Black Lance told him that the Agency guards intended to confiscate the carcase.

'That meat isn't going anywhere,' Wes announced as he placed himself between it and the horsemen.

'It was killed illegally,' Lame Dog answered.

'Even if this is part of the Sioux Reservation there is no restriction on hunting here. As a guest of Pawnee Killer I killed that animal. It is mine and it stays in this camp.' Lame Dog sat stoically astride his pony as though awaiting his instruction to be carried out, expecting the dead deer to be slung across his pony's rear quarters. Wes was equally implacable. 'If Mr Archer has a different viewpoint I'll argue it out with him when I meet him.'

When the guards had ridden away, the village women set to work on the carcase before it became the subject of further argument. Wes remounted the pinto and with Black Lance in attendance, rode north along the bank of the tributary towards the Cheyenne

River. It took less than an hour to reach a larger village. Here, high tepees were outnumbered by timber huts. Men sat outside many of these houses, wrapped in blankets, and displaying little interest in their surroundings. The dark faces showed the same degree of uncertainty that was apparent on those among the tepees of Pawnee Killer's village. When Wes passed by, however, more than one pair of eyes followed his progress to the centre of the encampment. News of the arrival of the famed Wiyaka Wakan had spread throughout the Agency families with inexplicable swiftness.

The women were almost unrecognizable as the spirited bodies he'd known in their normal, nomadic environment. Those busy, buckskin-clad bodies epitomized the life of the village; always working, always chattering and eager to laugh. Now they were drab and sullen, their clothes no better than shabby wool castoffs and their faces reflecting either some horror they'd left behind or the deprivation that was to be their future. Passing one of the tepees, Wes's attention was caught by the activity of an old woman who was kneeling at her work. She had a bowl which she was twisting from side-to-side to enable her to inspect the contents. It reminded Wes of miners he'd seen panning for gold in a river, washing the earth in a riddle hoping to find nuggets or gold dust in the bottom. He stopped and asked Black Lance what she was doing.

'It is her corn ration,' the Ogallalah told him. 'She has been thrifty. Most families have used up their supply.'

77

'Why is she doing that with it?'

'She will grind it but must first remove the dirt.'

It was at that point that Wes espied the sack that lay at the woman's side and recognized the peculiar red-ink government stamp on the bottom. It was the same mark as the one on the sack that Jenny had shown him the night before and which was now tied behind his saddle with the few belongings he'd brought with him. He dismounted and, to the woman's consternation, picked up the sack. He spent a moment assuring her that it wasn't his intention to steal it. The scowl on her face showed she had no trust in his words but subdued by the assurances of Black Lance, she ceased her harangue while Wes inspected the contents.

There was little in the bag. At first glance, Wes estimated there was probably enough to make another serving of the corn meal that the women prepared with whatever edible roots they could harvest. He dug into the bag but when he withdrew it, his hand wasn't full of corn. There was as much dirt as grain in the sack, an abundance of soil, grit and dirt, like floor sweepings.

Appalled by the discovery and by Black Lance's testimony that about a third of the contents of every sack was dirt, Wes remounted and made a bee line for the Agency offices which were part of a compound in the centre of the settlement. Together with the long, low, log-built administration building, there were two storehouses, stables and corrals. Big Mouth was on the veranda in front of the administration building as Wes and Black Lance approached, and was joined by Lame

Dog and a tall American before they reached the hitching rail.

The American was bare-headed and jacketless, his sleeves were rolled up as though he'd been interrupted in the execution of some task but he had a lit pipe clasped in his mouth indicating he hadn't been doing anything too strenuous. He had thick, wild hair and bushy eyebrows over bright blue eyes. He removed the pipe from his mouth, smiled and greeted his visitor.

'The boys tell me you are Medicine Feather, the famous Wes Gray. I'm Horace Archer, the Agent here at Cheyenne River.' When Wes looked at the 'boys' it was clear that they weren't pleased to see him. Their expressions were grim, tight-lipped and unsmiling. The American laughed. 'Don't mind them,' he told Wes, 'they take their work seriously and are a bit put-out because they lost a bit of authority when you baulked them over the dead deer. There are rules that need to be observed in order to keep the peace. While there are still hostile groups abroad who might incite reservation Indians back to war and raids, firearms are banned. Anyone discovered with a rifle is imprisoned and any animal shot is illegal game, therefore confiscated.'

'I killed the animal,' Wes told him. 'It was a gift to the people who gave me shelter and who wouldn't be starving if they were allowed to hunt their own food or if the supplies they received were in keeping with the promises that were made when the treaty was signed.'

'I know where your sympathies lie, Mr Gray, and

79

believe me, we're all trying to do our best for these people, but I don't think the Sioux here have any cause for complaint. Perhaps there are occasions when supplies arrive later than expected but that's due to the perils of weather and transportation. We feed them as swiftly as possible.'

'But the goods are spoiled,' Wes told him. 'If underweight grain sacks are being topped up with grit and dirt then I have no doubt that other tricks are being used to under-supply the people here. I've seen the shabby and thin clothes and blankets that have been their only protection against the harsh winter and I'm told that the cattle which are their major source of meat are scrawny and infected. The people in your charge are suffering, Mr Archer. What are you doing about it?'

Horace Archer remained diplomatic. 'You've got a list of grievances there, Mr Gray, but are they genuine? Look,' he pointed at the corrals, 'empty. All the cattle have been taken and eaten.'

'And many of the people have become sick and weakened by what they consumed.'

'What proof have you of that?'

'Perhaps the doctor assigned to the Agency can tell us how busy he's been during the winter.'

'I can only give the supplies that are delivered,' Horace Archer said with diminishing friendliness.

'That's true, but it is your job to safeguard the health of the people here. Have you reported the poor quality of the goods that are being delivered? Expressed any concern?'

'I have no concerns. These people grumble because they lost the war, not because they are hungry or cold. Feed them too well and they'll be running wild again. The government wants the benefits of the land, Mr Gray, it needs to be put to its best use and we can't let a few primitive people hold back the progress.'

'Then treat them in the way proscribed by the treaty. Any future uprising will be caused by your treatment, not the persuasion of Sitting Bull if he ever comes back this side of the border.' With that said, Wes and Black Lance turned their horses and rode away.

Horace Archer watched them go, his brow creased with concern. He was worried. First that old man had been snooping around and protesting about the treatment of the Indians here at the Agency and now it was Wes Gray. Crackaway had been trouble enough but he'd been dealt with. However, if his reputation was to be believed, Wes Gray was a different matter. Something had to be done. 'Lame Dog,' he said, 'I want you to take a message across the river to John Lord.'

SEVEN

Wes Gray re-crossed the Missouri then demanded a sustained run from the pinto. He was anxious to meet up with the supply train which included Rafe Leeward's wagon before they got too far from the Spearpoint cattle pens. Wes wanted to see for himself the cattle that had been earmarked for the Sioux Agency. Black Lance had told him that the previous herd had consisted of beeves unsuitable for consumption. Horace Archer, on the other hand, had denied that. Wes had no reason to doubt either man. The Indian Agent had been curt after listening to Wes's accusations but he hadn't changed his story, and Wes acknowledged that Horace Archer's reaction was probably no different to what his own would have been in similar circumstances. But the poverty of the reservation people couldn't be denied either and that, Wes knew, was neither the right way to treat those defeated people nor the intention that had been expressed by the policy-makers. If the Indians were being cheated then their plight needed to be disclosed and the culprits discovered. This, he thought, had been Crackaway's quest, and if it had led to his death then his murderers needed to pay for their crime.

For an instant, as he approached the split in the trail where the left-hand fork climbed away towards Palmersville, Wes thought he saw movement in the high ground, a glimpse of blue that might have been the clothing of a distant rider. But Palmersville wasn't his current destination. His route continued along the low, riverside road for a few more miles until he reached the east cut to Spearpoint. Although he was always cautious of other riders he had no reason to be suspicious of a traveller on another road nor the time to waste investigating. The wagons waiting at Council Bluffs were always his first concern.

Up above, however, that other traveller had rested his pony after its climb and observed the galloping horseman below. A fleeting thought crossed his mind and he reached for the rifle that was sheathed below his leg. With one well-aimed bullet he could return to the Agency, the need to deliver the message would have been removed and Archer would surely reward him with one of the new Winchester rifles he so admired.

Like many of his people, Lame Dog had not welcomed the refugees of the western bands when they first straggled into the region of the Cheyenne and Grand Rivers. It was generally agreed that they would bring with them their grievances and war-like ways.

83

His people, the Santee, had been settled in this territory for twenty years, living in peace and adopting the ways of the Americans. Now they were farmers, growing crops on their own strips of land. However, contrary to his expectations, the arrival of the Ogallalah and Hunkpapa had become a good thing for Lame Dog. He didn't like them or trust them, but since accepting the position of Agency guard, his wealth had increased and his standing within the community had grown. His authority over the newcomers was a power he enjoyed, gloating over the fact that warriors who had won glory along the Greasy Grass were now subjugated to his commands.

His willingness to repress the spirit of the insurgents produced a rise in his worth to Agent Archer and he soon became his right-hand man. Accordingly, rewards followed, small privileges progressed to additional payments and choice goods from the supplies that were intended for the bereft western Sioux. It was a situation that he was anxious to maintain. One threat to it had been dashed by the message he'd carried to John Lord regarding the old *wasicun*, but now the threat was renewed by the arrival of Wiyaka Wakan. His interference could spark resistance among the new arrivals.

Lame Dog was disappointed when Wes Gray didn't veer on to the uphill trail. He had assumed that the scout's destination was Palmersville and that he would come within range of his rifle before he was ever aware that he was in a gunman's sights. Now, he could only watch with frustration as the white man raced past the fork on the trail below. An unsuccessful shot would not only be a forewarning of the threat to his life but also point to the Agency as the source of his danger. Lame Dog lowered his rifle, returned it to its scabbard and pressed his heels against the flanks of his pony. The message would have to be delivered and the task of killing Wiyaka Wakan undertaken by white men in Palmersville.

Five hundred head of cattle had been hustled out of the Spearpoint pens early that morning, had then been chivvied around the outskirts of the town and led on to the wide expanse of plain that was the first stage of the journey to the Missouri. The weather was good and the way ahead free of hazards. The seven men in the crew of which Tad Carter was leader, would ease the cattle along to preserve their good condition. Even so, they expected to cover fifteen miles before sundown, the intention being to bed them down close to the funnel that led into the gap between the first high mounds of the grassy uplands.

For a man who'd endured the hardships of the Goodnight-Loving trail, this current undertaking was no challenge. Tad Carter, riding at the head of the herd, would get the cattle to their destination without breaking a sweat. His mind was occupied with a more troubling problem. He'd ridden with Clem Oates for several years and knew him to be as tough as any range rider he'd ever come across, but last night, when he'd shown up at the Yellow Mountain saloon in

Spearpoint, he'd been a frightened man. With wide, staring eyes, he'd described the effort to bushwhack Wes Gray which had resulted in the cruel deaths of Tom Petit and Texas Pete. He'd shot him, Clem had assured Tad, probably dead, but he hadn't gone back to make sure of the kill and Tad wasn't convinced he was telling the truth. The only thing he knew for certain was that Clem was gripped by fear; had lost his nerve. He'd watched as his companion had poured rotgut from a bottle and thrown it down his throat like so much water, impervious, it seemed, to its harshness and foul taste.

Tad recalled the fight in the saloon at Palmersville, remembered the stony expression on the face above him as he was pinned against a table with the point of a wicked hunting knife at his throat. It was the face of a man who had killed and would kill again when necessary. He could believe Clem's description of Texas Pete hanging from a tree and the gutting of Tom Petit with that same knife. An unexpected sensation that death was close at hand swept over Tad and he shouted an angry order at a trail-hand just to shake away the uncomfortable feeling. He hoped Wes Gray was dead. If he wasn't he would kill him on sight; he couldn't afford to give him any opportunity to shoot first.

From a high grassy dome, Wes Gray could see the dust of the herd as it made its slow progress in his direction. In front, perhaps a mile ahead so that the only dust they had to eat was their own, was a string of

86

high-sided wagons pulled by six-horse teams. Spare horses were tied to the tail-rail of some of the wagons in case of accidents along the trail, but a full remuda for the short drive to the Indian reservation and a wrangler or two to keep them on course had been deemed unnecessary. One of the wagons, Wes decided, would belong to Rafe Leeward. He would like to inspect the goods in those wagons, find out what was being delivered to the people of the Cheyenne River Agency. To satisfy his curiosity he nudged the pinto forward then let it pick its own way down the hillside to the grassy meadow below.

Rafe Leeward was three wagons back in the ten-long string and he'd recognized the pinto when it was some distance away. When they were within hailing distance he greeted Wes. The scout pulled his mount around in order to ride alongside the wagon. He wanted to know when they would reach the Agency.

'Two days,' Rafe told him. 'We'll cross the river tomorrow then it's a straight run after that.'

'What are you carrying?' Wes had allowed his eyes to roam over the stock in the back of the cart. There were boxes and kegs and soft bundles as well as bags and sacks which were piled high at the rear.

'Foodstuffs, tools and clothing. Regular commodities.'

'I hope it's better quality than the last shipment. The people over there are starving.'

'You've been on the reservation?' Rafe was clearly surprised by the other's freedom of movement.

'I've been,' he said, 'and they need those supplies

as soon as possible.'

Rafe's mind suddenly caught up with Wes Gray's previous words. 'What do you mean, better quality? We take what we get. It all comes from the government stores in Cincinnati.'

Wes had seen some sacks at the back of the wagon that were marked with the now familiar red government stamp. He hoisted himself on to the back of the wagon straight from the saddle. Rafe Leeward shouted in protest and a rider from the head of the column swung his horse around so that he could investigate the commotion.

'Hey you,' he yelled. 'Get down from there.'

Wes ignored him and hauled one of the sacks forward. Something about it had excited his interest. It had been sewn along the top but not with any precision. Wes's immediate impression was that the sack had been opened and hastily re-stitched.

'Who are you?' demanded the man on horseback. 'What are you doing on that wagon?'

Wes ignored him. 'What's in here?' he asked Rafe.

'Grain,' was the answer then immediately, Rafe spoke to the other man. 'This is Wes Gray, Hugo, the man they call Medicine Feather.'

The fame of the frontiersman didn't appease Hugo, who was the leader of the supply train. 'That's government property you're interfering with. I'd advise you to get off that wagon now.'

Wes barely threw the man a glance. 'I don't think I'm the first to have interfered with it,' he declared, showing the uneven line of stitches. With unexpected swiftness he pulled his knife from its embroidered sheath and prepared to slice across the top of the sack.

Yells of outrage issued from both Rafe and Hugo. A pistol appeared in the latter's hand pointed directly at Wes Gray's chest. 'Mister,' he said, 'that sack has a government stamp on it and it's my job to get it and everything else in these wagons to their destination. I'll shoot you like a common road-agent if you put the smallest nick in it.'

Wes Gray didn't like people pointing guns at him; he felt the weight of the knife in his hand and considered the possibility of hurling it into Hugo's chest more quickly than the other could pull the trigger. But he refrained from violence – it was possible that the man was innocent of any plot to cheat the Sioux of their rightful goods.

'Does the government know that these sacks have been opened?' Wes asked.

'Not by me or any of these drivers,' Hugo replied. 'We just deliver what arrives.'

'But you supervise the loading of the wagons?'

'No. That's done in Palmersville. I don't see them until the cattle arrive and we're ready to leave.'

'So you don't know the condition of the goods you're transporting.'

'No need to know. My job is just to get them there.'

'The Sioux are starving because they are receiving fouled goods. I want to know if this cargo, too, has been spoiled.'

'Not my business to interfere.' Hugo had consignment notes that had been duly completed. Any discrepancy or complaint concerning the items delivered was a matter between the Cheyenne River Agent and the Bureau of Indian Affairs, and Wes Gray had no authority to stop the wagons nor to examine the cargo. They had a few more miles to complete before sundown and couldn't afford to delay any longer. 'The cattle are getting closer,' he added, 'the drovers will be wondering why we've stopped.'

He was right. Rafe, standing to look back across the meadow, pointed at a rider bustling forward, the hoofs of his galloping bronco kicking up dust and stones as it advanced.

'What's the trouble?' the cowboy asked as he reined in beside Hugo. 'Tad wants to know why you've stopped. He says we can cover another mile or two before bedding them down for the night.'

'We're moving on now,' Hugo assured him. 'Mr Busybody here,' he indicated Wes in the back of the high wagon, 'has taken an interest in the goods we're carrying. But it's time for him to go.' He looked up at Wes and spoke to him. 'Like I say, Mr Gray, you've got no authority to interfere with goods we're carrying so I suggest you get back on your horse and don't interfere with government property again.'

Wes didn't want to get into any kind of ruckus with the teamsters, they were simply doing a job of work, but he was sure that if they were opened he would find the sacks had been plundered of half their contents and topped up with dirt to make up the lost weight. He was keen to inspect all the goods in the wagon, find out if the other foodstuffs had been tampered with in some way and if the remainder of the cargo was suitable for its purpose. If the government was sincere in its efforts to convert the Sioux into farmers then the tools it was sending on to the reservation needed to be suitable for the job. He clambered on to the pinto from the back of the wagon.

The cow-herder was watching him closely. Wes Gray's name had been on everyone's lips since the beginning of the trip and, noting the frontiersman's buckskin clothing and the long eagle feather attached to his hat band, quickly deduced that that was the identity of the man now astride the pinto. The fight in the Palmersville saloon had been a major topic of conversation over the past couple of days, although not while Tad Carter was in the vicinity. Still, he had no doubt that Tad would be interested in the news that the man who had got the best of him and Clem Oates was the cause of the current delay and showing great interest in the goods that were being transported to the reservation. 'I'll tell Tad you're pushing on,' he said to Hugo then, with a lingering look at Wes Gray, turned his horse and raced back towards the herd that was more than half a mile distant.

The man's interest in him hadn't escaped Wes Gray and he knew his presence would be reported to those riding with the cattle. The man had dropped the name Tad when speaking with Hugo so Wes assumed that Tad Carter was with the trailing herd. It seemed likely that one day there would be a reckoning between them. It had almost occurred at the cemetery gates but Jenny Trantor's arrival had put a halt to that. Perhaps when the cowboy reported back Tad would come looking for him, but according to Bob Best, that wasn't Tad's style. John Lord's man preferred to be the possessor of an unfair advantage. For the moment, it suited Wes to avoid a conflict. His main purpose was to find someone with the authority to check those wagons before they got across the Missouri. He wasn't sure such a person existed but he had to try. He took his leave of Rafe Leeward and cut away up the hillside.

Once over the brow of the hill and beyond the sight of those below he reined to a halt, his intention to investigate the contents of the sacks simply delayed, not abandoned. He dismounted, removed his hat to lessen the possibility of being spotted from the plain below and crouched in the grass to observe the scene. If, when he got the cowboy's report, Tad sent out men to hunt for him, he wanted to know about it. However, his observations put an end to that possibility. There were only seven men with the herd so until they were bedded down for the night everyone was needed to keep the herd together and moving. One man, probably Tad Carter, led the way forty or fifty yards ahead of the herd. Two men rode drag to hustle the stragglers and there was a point and swing rider at either side to keep the herd tight. Nothing in the way the cattle moved suggested to Wes that they were anything but A1 beef, but from his high point and with a view obscured by high rising dust, it was hard to be certain. He needed to get closer but for that he had to wait for darkness. Tad Carter would be on the lookout for him now that he was aware of his interest in the wagons.

Wes Gray had long since learned the lesson of patience, that it paid to wait for favourable conditions before committing to action and although, on this occasion, the delay was eating into the time he had to spare before reaching Council Bluffs, he didn't allow it to become a consideration that affected his decision. He waited on the hillside and watched as those below settled down for a night camp. The herd was halted four hundred yards short of where the wagons had been arranged in a long oval. By the time darkness came, fires had been lit, a meal prepared and night guards posted. Despite Rafe Leeward's declaration that the wagons and cattle travelled together to ward off robbers, Wes knew that the major task of the night herders was to keep the cattle settled. They were nervous critters, easily spooked by the scent of a wolf or the grumble of a grizzly bear. The herders themselves would be more asleep than awake in the saddle as they made an occasional circle of the herd.

He made his move when he figured that all but the two cattle guards were in their blankets. After he picketed the pinto in a grove of trees he descended the hillside on foot. Having accompanied the warriors of his Arapaho village on raids against the Crow and Shoshone, he was able to approach the cattle herd undetected. He paused in a patch of long grass while one of the herders rode past with his head slumped forward on his chest. Perhaps because it caught Wes's scent as it passed within a handful of strides, the horse snorted and startled its rider into wakefulness. He stopped, cast his eyes over the sleeping cattle then, content that all was well, moved on again. Wes figured he had thirty minutes to check out the herd before the far rider had circled around to this point.

Crouching, Wes moved silently among the sleeping beasts. It didn't take him long to decide that they were prime beef animals. He wasn't an expert on cattle but he suspected that these were a cross-breed with Herefords in their lineage. They were full-bodied, as Sheriff Johnson in Palmersville had told him. Good stock, not the old, skinny, perhaps infected cattle, he confessed, that he'd expected to find. He knew he should be pleased that the Sioux would soon have meat for their pots but he couldn't shake away the images he carried of the suffering people at the Cheyenne River Agency. He determined to investigate the wagons; perhaps he would find something there that would produce evidence to support the Sioux claims of false dealing from the government.

Under cover of darkness, the distance to the wagons was easily covered. Wes's long-legged lope devoured the distance and robbed him of little energy. He kept his eyes open for the positions of the circling night herders but they neither saw nor heard him. For added security, to lessen the possibility of a chance sighting by either of the horsemen, Wes worked his way to the farthest end of the oval before selecting a wagon to investigate. Men were sleeping under some of the wagons but he could see many forms settled around the remnants of the two fires that had been the focal point for the night-time meals, card games and discussions. Wes hoped that no one had chosen to sleep in the wagon he selected.

It was a good choice. Like Rafe Leeward's it contained a variety of goods and although there was little light to aid his search he was soon convinced that the sacks in this wagon had, like those in Rafe's, been opened and re-stitched. But it was when he moved aside a bundle of blankets that he made his major discovery. A row of small kegs were jammed against the wagon's front board and under the driver's seat. The harsh smell of cheap whiskey assailed Wes's sensitive nostrils. The sale of whiskey to Indians was strictly prohibited and its transportation on to reservation land as part of approved government supplies would not be condoned. Clearly, the goods that were being delivered were not those designated by the Bureau of Indian Affairs.

For Wes, the discovery simplified matters. If he could get a message to a military post then the army would intercept the wagons before the goods were delivered to the Agency, and John Lord would have a lot of questions to answer. He was about to slip back over the side of the wagon when the sound of a fast approaching horse carried to him.

A voice shouted from somewhere within the camp. 'Rider coming. Rider coming.'

Men were stirring all around. Two torches were quickly lit from the embers of the dying fires and held aloft to cast a light for the incoming horseman. They positioned themselves at the gap between the next wagons from the one in which Wes still waited. He lay flat and still, hoping that the dancing flames wouldn't choose some ill moment to illuminate him.

Tad Carter was flanked by two armed men when he reached the spot where the horseman had halted. Although gruff in his acknowledgement of the new arrival, it seemed to Wes that the visitor wasn't unexpected. If Carter was annoyed by the interruption to his sleep, his words didn't betray it.

'Where's Clem?'

'He sent me instead.' There was a hint of anger in his voice, as though he should be sleeping at this hour, not riding across the open range in moonlight.

'Everything OK?' Tad asked.

'Apart from Clem jumping at every sound and movement. Something's got him as nervous as a new colt.'

'It's that squaw man and Clem might have reason to be worried. He was hanging around the wagons a couple of hours ago. He's gone now, probably to Palmersville. Tell Clem to give that place a wide berth for a while.'

'Everything OK for tomorrow?' the rider asked.

'Sure. All set. Step down and have some coffee before you go back.'

When they'd gone to sit by a fire Wes knew he had to take the opportunity to leave. There were men awake all around the compound and he risked discovery at every moment. He slipped over the side of the wagon but no sooner had his feet touched the ground than he heard the soft footfalls of a walking horse and a voice shouting, 'Hey, you. What are you doing there?'

EIGHT

The presence of the rider surprised Wes. He'd assumed that the activity occasioned by the horseman's arrival had been restricted to within the wagon ring and had waited until everyone nearby had gone back to their bedroll or to take their share from the coffeepot simmering at the fire. He had no way of knowing how long the rider had been behind him or had been watching him but clearly his shouted challenge had been heard and men were coming to investigate. Quick action was required if he was to evade capture and not become Tad Carter's prisoner.

The rider, a youngish fellow, was leaning forward, both hands resting on the saddle-horn so that his follow-up question, 'Who are you?' seemed more like a polite enquiry than a threatening challenge. It took Wes less than a moment to realize that the lad wasn't even wearing a side-arm, which he knew wasn't unusual. Many cow-herders found a pistol in a holster was a handicap when working a herd, especially at night when the aim was to keep the animals quiet. A sudden gunshot, even if accidental, could send a herd running for miles.

Wes took advantage of the lad's naivety. He flung his arms in the air, startling the horse which flung its head in the air as it stepped backwards. The rider shifted in the saddle, took a tighter hold on the reins and tried to settle the animal. Wes jumped forward, grabbed two handfuls of the rider's shirt and pulled him to the ground. A mixture of sounds now filled the once quiet night. The lad's yells and the horse's snorts were joined by the excited enquiries of the men at the other side of the wagons. Wes ignored them all, grasped the saddle-horn and swung himself on to the horse's back. Lying low along the animal, he was racing away from the wagons before any attempt could be made to stop him.

By the time anyone was in position to fire a shot it was clear that to do so would be a waste of ammunition. The fleeing figure was lost in the darkness. The description provided by the un-horsed herder left no room for doubt as to the identity of their visitor and, when the uncovered whiskey kegs were discovered, Tad cursed Wes Gray.

He drew his four closest allies aside. 'I want that man dead,' he told them. 'He knows too much. Scour these hills and shoot on sight.'

'He could be anywhere,' someone said, 'and he'll be miles away by now.'

'Perhaps not,' Tad told him. 'He fled on one of our ponies but I'll warrant he comes back for his own horse. It must be picketed somewhere close. If you find it you can ambush him when he returns. Take no chances,' he warned everyone, 'he's dangerous. There'll be a reward for the man who kills him.'

Many minutes passed while guns were checked and horses saddled before two pairs of man-hunters rode out to search the swells and troughs of the surrounding territory. However, they weren't the first to leave the perimeter of the camp ground. Clem's messenger preceded them, carrying the good news that the plan was on schedule, but also the bad news that Wes Gray was alive and at large somewhere close. At a steady pace, he headed towards the funnel through which the cattle and wagons were due to pass shortly after daybreak.

When he'd made his escape, Wes Gray's first thought had been to gain a good head start before a pursuit could be organized. In the darkness he'd stuck to the low meadow land, trusting to luck that the horse wouldn't stumble as it galloped across the rugged terrain. He'd ridden for about ten minutes when he spotted a stand of trees off to his right and steered the horse towards them. He was considering his next move, whether to return to the hillside spot where he'd left the pinto and ride for Spearpoint from where he'd be able to telegraph details of the illegal whiskey load to Fort Pierre, or hang about in the hills and watch the activities that unfolded around the supply train in the morning.

Logic, he knew, dictated the former; the army would need the information at the earliest moment if they were to intercept the wagons before they reached the Cheyenne River Agency. Deep down, however, instinct told him that whatever was meant to occur when the wagons continued their journey it would not be to the benefit of the people across the river. He wanted to be on hand to foil the plan or, if that wasn't possible to gain some evidence to use against them. He was only one man, but that was the way he worked best.

He was still among the trees when he heard the steady thrum of hoof beats. After a few moments he was able to see the silhouette of a single rider. It took only a moment to assess that this was the messenger returning to Clem and that following him might provide the information Wes was looking for. It wouldn't be easy, it was a clear night and the darkness would soon be giving way to the first light of the coming dawn, but Wes had already decided that the risk of discovery was outweighed by the knowledge he might gain.

In fact, the risk was very soon reduced because the rider rode unerringly towards the funnel-like opening that led between two high mounds and was lost in its darkness. Wes halted and listened. The rider hadn't stopped, the pace of the hoof beats hadn't altered. Wes urged his horse along the long, twisting valley. After twenty minutes of riding he reached the mouth of another, narrower valley, cutting away north-westerly. Again he halted and listened and now the horse's steps were slow, distinct. It was walking; now and then its iron shoes struck hard rock as the ground rose to a higher level.

101

Gut feeling told Wes he was close to Clem's camp. He was pondering whether to leave the horse at the mouth of the valley and progress on foot when an unexpected sound reached his ears. He turned, looked back towards the plain land that he'd left behind. Nothing, all was still, but he would have been surprised if it had been different; it wasn't possible that the cattle had been driven so far in such a short space of time. But then he heard it again. The lowing of a cow and this time he knew it was coming from farther along the branch-off valley. He dismounted, tethered the horse to a bush and began the trek up the valley.

A fire burned brightly, its unusually high flames marking the position of the camp before Wes was within half a mile of it. With his usual stealth, he climbed the hillside and found a position from which he could observe those below. Close to the fire, three men were sleeping with their heads on their saddles. Another two were talking to the rider who hadn't yet dismounted. Wes recognized one of the men as Clem Oates whose agitated movements conveyed the fact that he'd just been told that Wes was not dead.

Beyond the camp were the cattle, not a small bunch but a herd equal in size to the one Wes had left behind on the open meadow. He moved deeper into the valley to get a closer look at the animals espying only one horseman in motionless vigil to watch over them. Avoiding the attention of the night-guard, Wes crept down the hillside and mingled with the sleeping cattle. One or two grunted in surprise as the frontiersman moved swiftly among them. The smell of kerosene hung around many of the animals, its use being a cheap and unpredictable cure for skin diseases and mange, and others showed evidence of crude remedies for screwworms and blowfly infestation. They were skinny animals and their suffering had deprived them of their true health and vigour. How some of them had survived the winter was a source of amazement to Wes.

It was clear to the frontiersman that once the supply train had passed through the main valley these beasts would replace the healthy critters that were currently following the wagons. Infected stock would be driven on to the reservation; the Sioux rations would consist of contaminated meat. If he was to prevent that then he knew he must work quickly. He lifted his head to see where the night-guard was positioned.

Man and horse hadn't moved since Wes had first moved in among the herd. It was probable that, like the cattle they'd been posted to watch over, they were asleep. Wes worked his way back to the fringe of the herd then edged closer to the mounted man. He selected a cow, kicked its rump then moved behind a nearby boulder. He knew enough about animals to predict what would happen next – what he wasn't sure about, however, was the reaction of the cowboy.

The offended cow bellowed and rose to its feet. Instinctively, its neighbours, governed by their inbred nervousness and alarmed by the possibility of a natural predator in their midst, followed suit. Within moments the disturbance had spread throughout the herd. Every animal was on its feet, snorting and milling around in wide-eyed anxiety.

The night-guard's horse, affected by the nervousness of the cattle, shook its head with a violent suddenness that startled its rider. But he was an experienced man and was instantly in control of the animal under him. He was also quick to identify the area where the commotion had begun. He moved his mount slowly, talking as he made his way around the perimeter of the herd. One of the beasts, he suspected, had picked up the scent of wild cat or wolf in the high ground. It would be reassured by his presence. It never to ceased amaze him how quickly these big beasts with their long horns could be spooked by the scent of a cat or a dog that was so small in comparison, nor how quickly they could be calmed by a horseman riding by. He drew his pistol but hoped he wouldn't have to use it. It would be a few minutes yet before they were resettled.

'Steady, steady,' he was cooing to the jumpy critters when, without warning, someone jumped on to the back of his horse, clamped a hand over his mouth and struck him solidly on the side of the head with a gun butt. With barely a murmur, he slipped from the saddle and lay still on the ground.

Wes rode back to the head of the herd, a position between the cattle and the campfire, then, accompanied by a series of 'Yip, yip,' yells, fired over their heads and sent them off in a stampede along the valley. He didn't know how long it was nor where it led, but he hoped it wasn't a dead-end canyon. He wanted them to run for miles and spread into the hills and adjoining valleys. Scattering them was the best option he had to prevent them replacing those prime animals that were truly intended for the Indians across the river. He could have chased them the other way, back into the valley where he'd left his borrowed horse, but that opened up the possibility of them merging with and contaminating the other herd. When they were in flight, Wes dismounted, slapped the animal's rear and sent it running after them. It wouldn't stop until the cattle did.

Around the campfire Clem and the men with whom he was talking had become aware of the unrest among the cattle. The gunshots brought the remainder from their bedrolls. The cause of the stampede and the reason for the gunshots were complete mysteries to Clem and the men. Long moments of confusion followed before the men were able to mount up and give chase but they knew that in the narrow valley they had no hope of getting ahead of the leaders. The cattle would run until exhausted and by then they would probably be widespread. It would take days to round them up into a herd again.

Clem didn't ride out with the rest of the crew; he stood with his back to the fire, looking into the night, listening to the rumble of running beeves and the men's diminishing shouts. Never before had he met with so many reversals of fortune. The fight in the saloon, the attempt to ambush the squaw man and now babysitting a herd of mangy cattle that would have provided a welcome bonus when the prime cattle were sold to the cattle buyer in Spearpoint.

105

What, he wondered, would Tad say? More importantly, what would John Lord do? Behind him the fire rustled, like the burning branches had collapsed and perhaps spread out of their circle. He turned to attend to it and instantly recoiled. Clem's mouth opened as though uttering a shout of fear, but no sound came forth. His eyes were fixed on the figure at the other side of the flames, a man in buckskin with a long feather in his hat.

'You wanted to kill me,' said Wes Gray, 'well here I am.'

Clem reached out a hand, a hapless, defensive gesture meant to convey a misunderstanding, a mistake, innocence, anything that would prevent the moment of death predicted by the cold stare in the other's eyes. 'No,' was all he said.

'You came after me without warning. Three against one. Well I'm giving you an even chance. Go for your gun.'

'No,' Clem said again. 'You'll kill me.'

'That's right. I'll kill you.' While talking Wes had had his thumbs tucked into his gunbelt. Now he let his hands fall away to hang loosely at his sides. 'Whenever you're ready.'

'It wasn't my idea to kill you.' Words tumbled out of Clem's mouth. 'It was Tad and Mr Lord.'

'Why?'

'Because you are a friend of the old man.'

'Crackaway!'

'Mr Lord didn't want you prying in his business.'

'You mean he doesn't want me to find out what

Crackaway discovered, that John Lord is stealing government supplies intended for the Sioux Agency across the river.'

Clem's shoulders sagged. He'd hoped to buy his life with information about John Lord's activities but Wes Gray it seemed already knew what was happening. The scout's following remark proved the hopelessness of the situation.

'Did Crackaway catch people filling grain sacks with dirt? Is that why he was killed?' Clem shook his head but Wes was sure that he wasn't denying the accusation. 'Was he dead before he was put in with the horse?'

'It was an accident,' pleaded Clem.

Wes was relentless. 'Who killed him?' he wanted to know. 'Was it you?'

Clem's only answer was a swift lick of his lips. He dismissed the urge to plead, to promise to leave the territory, have nothing more to do with the swindling ploys conducted by John Lord, but he knew it was too late. There was no hint of mercy in those eyes that were fixed on him. They had barely blinked once since the start of the confrontation. His only avenue of escape was by killing the scout. Without a moment's hesitation, hoping to catch the renowned frontiersman unawares, his hand dropped to the butt of his pistol. It got no farther. Wes Gray drew with unmatchable speed and put three bullets in Clem's heart. He sank to his knees and pitched forward into the flames. Wes left him there to burn.

*

After replacing the three spent cartridges, Wes set off in his customary ground-covering lope, back to the place where he'd tethered the horse. Thoughts of pursuit by Clem's companions were dismissed from his mind; they wouldn't have heard the gunshots above the thunderous sound of running cattle and were unlikely to return to the campsite before the sun was spreading light into the valley. However his senses were still acute and he suddenly stopped, lay flat on the ground and waited. There was movement ahead, something, someone moving slowly. A stone rolled and slithered, iron scratched against rock and a high-toned whisper of sound reached him as metal rubbed against metal. Bridle rings, he determined and wondered for a moment if the horse had slipped its tethering. Instinct prompted caution and he continued to wait. Then a voice carried to him, an injudicious uttering that carried clearly to Wes.

'That's a big fire. It must be Clem's camp.'

'Shut up.' The second man's command was terse, an indication that he was aware that sounds carried a long way in these valleys and that noise betrayed location.

The first man failed to pick up on his colleague's warning. 'Do you think the shots came from there? Will it be the squaw man?'

'Be quiet,' hissed the other. 'He could be anywhere around here. We won't get the bonus Tad promised by getting ourselves killed.'

In a moment, their shapes became apparent to Wes. They were close together, one half a length ahead of the other. They were carrying their rifles across their laps, ready to shoot at the first opportunity. He lay still, and even though they passed within five yards they were ignorant of his presence. It was apparent that they weren't experienced trackers, they hadn't even found the horse he'd left near the mouth of this narrow valley, but they'd come to kill him and were hoping to make a profit from the deed. He couldn't allow that. If he chose, he could return to his horse and be well on the way to Spearpoint before the duo had got over the shock of pulling Clem's body out of the fire, but he knew he had to make them suffer for their mercenary action.

The smell of burning flesh had been in their nostrils for some minutes before the man reached the fire. From their saddles they looked around the site, confused by the absence of any crew.

'Where is everyone?' asked the younger, talkative rider, 'and what have they been cooking?'

The other rider stepped down, his face registering curiosity, his attention captured by a pair of boots left warming by the flames. Three yards short of the fire he stopped, and gazed at the body that was burning black before him. The boots were the only items of the man's attire that had not been destroyed. He turned aside, horrified by the scene before him, but he knew he had to pull the body off the fire. It was the civilized thing to do. He put his rifle on the ground, bent and grabbed a boot. It was hot but not unbearable.

'Come and help me,' he called over his shoulder to

his partner. 'That savage has thrown somebody on the fire. I think it's Clem.' He tugged again, budging the blackened carcase a few inches. It gave him the opportunity to gain a better hold on the dead man's legs. Behind him he heard a thump, like a body hitting the ground. He half turned but a rope suddenly fell over his shoulders and pinned his arms to his side. A sharp tug pulled him off his feet and he was dragged backwards.

Yelling, he tried to stop the indignity by scuffing his feet in the ground, but it was to no avail. He flipped over on to his stomach and in that moment saw his tormentor. On the back of his companion's horse sat the man in buckskin he'd left the wagons to kill. The tables had turned; he was entirely at the other's mercy. His friend, young Hank, was a still lump on the ground, either dead or unconscious. He watched as the scout secured the rope to the saddle-horn, like he'd secured a yearling for branding, then dismounted.

Wes Gray took the rope from the other saddle and trussed up the younger man whom he'd rendered unconscious with a blow from his pistol. He propped him against a tree then did the same to the first man. When that was done he threw water in the younger man's face to revive him then spoke to both. 'You call me a savage but it is you who are hunting me. I've done you no harm but for money you are willing to kill me. Is it not right then that I take your lives?'

'Please don't, mister,' said Hank, the younger man, 'we won't do it again.'

110

The other refused to beg for his life although it seemed that it was now approaching its end. The man in buckskin had pulled an evil-looking hunting knife from the scabbard at his side.

'No. You won't do it again. You will leave this territory. Go south or east. Never return. You will carry my mark wherever you go. If I see you again I will kill you.'

He sliced a deep 'V' into the left cheek of each man. Through the awful pain they heard his voice.

'I am not a savage. I am not a squaw man. I am Medicine Feather, brother of the Arapaho and friend of the Sioux.'

NINE

Amid the dark, high-ground shadows, Wes dismounted. The pink light of dawn was reaching across the meadowland below. The cattle were already on their feet, lowing with impatience, anxious to be moving because they needed water and perhaps had woken with the smell of the distant Missouri in their nostrils. There was activity, too, within the circle. Bedrolls had been stashed away, breakfast eaten and teams were being harnessed to their wagons. Tad Carter was issuing instructions, ordering some men who had travelled as wagon guards to saddle spare cowponies. Until the men he'd sent out to hunt down the troublesome scout had returned they would have to do the work of drovers. Some of them grumbled but no one disobeyed.

Wes watched the preparations for a few moments, resting after the long, cautious ride from the other camp fire. The knowledge that Tad had offered a bonus to the hunters for killing him had planted the thought in his head that others might be abroad with the same incentive. So he had ridden back along the valley and into the meadowland with his senses keen to detect the slightest sound, sight or smell that was extraordinary to his surroundings. There had been no incidents, but Wes remained vigilant. He was hungry but would have to wait until he was reunited with the pinto before eating. There was pemmican in the saddle-bags which his Arapaho wife, Little Feather, had prepared for his journey to Council Bluffs.

By his reckoning, he'd left the pinto a mile east of where he now stood, at a spot roughly adjacent to the back of the herd. It was a distance he could cover on foot in less than ten minutes. He tied the reins to the saddle-horn and slapped the horse's rump to let it know it was free to roam. In a while it would rejoin the supply train. With luck it would approach them from the front, before they got underway, by which time he'd be behind them and heading for Spearpoint on his rested pinto.

The morning was becoming lighter with each step he took, but he took advantage of every bit of cover and shadow as he loped across the hillside. At strategic points he stopped and assessed the situation. He watched the trees for signs of ambush, listened to the birds for unnatural chatter and raised his head to catch any uncommon scent carried in the morning air. Satisfied, he moved on again.

From the cover of a low bush, he caught sight of the pinto as it grazed on the short hillside grass. Its neck was stretched out in that familiar manner, every movement languid, as though disinterested in anything but filling its stomach. As it ate, it turned until it was facing the bush behind which Wes Gray studied the surrounding area. The horse had seen him, looked at him although it didn't forsake its interest in the grass at its feet. Then it lifted its head, not startled, but slowly, as it had done the morning they'd quit Palmersville when it was letting him know about the riders in the hills. Now he was sure it was warning him of another danger. Someone else was hidden among the trees, waiting to ambush him when he stepped out to claim the horse.

Wes remained still, scanned each bush, tree and rock that could conceal a man but nothing showed. He looked high and low but there was neither an unexpected movement nor unnecessary sound. The half-light and deep shadows which provided help to his progress were also a hindrance to his ability to find a bushwhacker. He lay on the ground and squirmed backwards, back among trees that gave him greater cover.

Crouching low, moving in short, swift stages of no more than ten steps, he circled the spot where the pinto was tethered. At the completion of each stage he examined the undergrowth, strained his eyes and ears for a tell-tale sign. He was almost directly opposite the place where he'd watched the pinto when he saw the man who was lying full length on the ground. The dark clothes he wore allowed him to blend into the shadows and, coupled with his stillness, had made detection of his presence almost impossible. His rifle was close to his side, which implied he wasn't aware

114

that Wes was close at hand. Wes drew his knife from its sheath and moved stealthily forward.

At that moment, somewhere behind Wes, a horse snickered.

The man on the ground half turned. 'Can't you keep them quiet, Pecos?' he said.

Wes, too, turned, looked back to see another man with two horses.

The second man yelled a warning, drew his pistol and fired two shots at the place where Wes had been standing.

The man on the ground rolled, gathered up his rifle but by the time he fired a shot he, too, was too late to hit the frontiersman.

Because he was already holding the knife in his right hand, Wes knew he couldn't beat to the draw the man with the horses. Instead, he moved swiftly, hurdling a fallen tree then rolling into some deep groundcover which took him out of sight of his two adversaries.

The man with the rifle fired four shells at the fallen tree, ripping out chunks that spiralled in the air. The second man, approaching from a different direction could see that Wes wasn't behind the trunk.

'He's not there,' he called. He sought refuge behind a high willow, peering first round one side then the other in a bid to see where the scout was holed up.

The man with the rifle signalled for his companion to circle behind the place they assumed Wes to be, try to catch him in a crossfire. As soon as the other began to move, the rifleman scuttled across to the fallen tree. He'd expected his advance to draw shots from the man they were trying to kill but nothing came. He rested the barrel of the rifle across the trunk so that his aim would be steady when the man called Medicine Feather was in his sights. The bonus money, he reckoned, belonged to Pecos and him.

But the manoeuvre was not a new tactic to Wes Gray. Enemies had tried to catch him in a crossfire on other occasions and he was still alive to tell the tale. Experience had taught him three things about such situations. Superiority of numbers often lulled adversaries into acts of carelessness, the best hope for survival was not to be where your enemies expected you to be when the trap was sprung, and always strike first.

The groundcover of low brush and forest ferns into which Wes had rolled after clearing the tree trunk hid the fact that the land sloped gently into a dell which gave him the freedom to move undetected away from spot where he seemed to have taken refuge. Knowing the location of his two assailants was an advantage. Although plunging deeper into the surrounding woodland to escape their guns might have been an obvious course of action, Wes chose to do the opposite. Slithering like a snake he made his way towards the circling man. He, Wes calculated, was the weak link. He anticipated sneaking up behind Wes and shooting him in the back. He wouldn't expect to be confronted by the man he was hunting.

The name Pecos had been uttered by the other

man before shots were fired and Wes watched him hurrying forward, stoop-shouldered, a token gesture to caution as he sought for his victim. Wes lay still, gripped his knife tightly, almost reluctant to slay such an unworthy opponent. But the man had shot at him – would do so again if he got the opportunity so couldn't be spared. Wes had been generous with the two at Clem's camp but he had captured them before they had had a chance to show their true intention. They hadn't attacked him in any way, so perhaps they never would have done. He wouldn't kill a man who hadn't tried to kill him first.

Pecos had the tracking skills of a grizzly bear. Wes could hear every footfall, every ragged wheeze as the man pushed aside fronds and branches, peering forward in the expectation of setting eyes on his victim.

'Pecos,' Wes whispered, so close behind that the other man felt his breath on his neck. Startled, Pecos turned, so surprised that he almost forgot he had a gun in his hand. It didn't matter. Wes thrust the big, cruel hunting knife into the other's chest, twisted it, then caught the man as he began to collapse to the ground. He wiped the blood off the blade on Pecos's shirt and returned it to its sheath. Then, with his pistol in his hand, he back-tracked the dead man's route to bring him round behind the first man.

Unlike Pecos, Wes moved as swiftly and softly as a shadow. He was a big man yet he had stalking skills that were the equal of any native tribesman. Learning to move with uncommon stealth had been essential to provide him with meat and to defeat his enemies. His latest enemy was currently prone a dozen yards from where he stood. The man was sighting along his rifle, which was resting across the felled tree trunk that Wes had earlier hurdled. He lifted his head, listening for a sound, expecting, Wes supposed, Pecos to begin firing shots that would either kill or flush Wes out of his hiding place.

'Pecos can't help you,' Wes said.

The man began to turn then stopped. The rifle was cocked, ready for firing, calculations were happening in his mind. Could he turn quickly enough to outshoot the man in buckskin? Would he expect him to discard his weapon and surrender? A look over his shoulder told him that the man had his arms hanging at his side, wasn't prepared to fire. He rolled on to his back and lifted his rifle with deadly intent.

Wes wasn't unprepared, it was the reaction he both expected and wanted. The scout's right arm bent at the elbow and his Colt roared twice. Both bullets found their mark and another man he'd never known lay dead at his feet. Wes had no sympathy for him, no regret that he'd been forced to kill him.

The pinto lifted its head as Wes approached and accepted the muzzle rub that was reward for the warning it had given. Wes climbed on to its back and turned it towards Spearpoint. At first, he let it run easy, let it find a rhythm until he felt it stretching out, eager to run hard. He was anxious to be clear of the herd. If the cattle weren't yet moving it was possible that the gunshots had been heard by those on the meadow below. In which case, riders might come to investigate. Besides, he didn't know how many men Tad Carter had sent against him; there could be others riding the hills hoping to reap a bonus by killing him.

He could hear the whistle of a train as he took the downward slope into Spearpoint and he could see its black smoke chuffing above the tops of the buildings. It was a timely guide because he figured the telegraph office would be part of the railway facilities. He avoided the main street, veered around the top end of the town until he encountered the rails, which he followed down to the depot. Beyond, there were two empty stockyards each of which looked capable of holding a thousand head of cattle. A few men were hovering near those pens watching the train that had just arrived at the platform. People had congregated at the trackside, not to board the train, merely curious about anyone who might be leaving or arriving in their town.

Wes dismounted at the corner of the station building, raising as many eyebrows by his backwoods appearance as the dandified rail travellers from the east. Wes ignored everyone and entered the station office. 'I need to send a telegraph message to Fort Pierre,' he told the clerk. 'It's urgent.'

He wrote his message and handed it to the clerk for transmission. 'How much is that?'

The clerk read the message, counting the words as he did so. When he was done he quoted a price but his eyes lifted over Wes's shoulders to catch the attention of a man who had followed the scout into the railway office. Wes had been too busy with pad and pencil stub to pay him any heed. He was dressed in a dark vest and jacket and wore a black derby on his head.

'Stranger in town,' he said, almost conversationally, but edged with presumptuousness.

'That's right.' Wes didn't like people prying into his business.

'Thought so. Saw you ride in. You looked like a man in a hurry. Always arouses my interest.'

'Not your concern,' Wes told him.

The man held out his hand to the clerk who handed over the form that Wes had completed.

'Hey,' Wes protested.

The man gently tugged aside the jacket lapel to reveal the tin star pinned to his waistcoat. 'This is my town. I like to know what's going on, Mr. . . ?'

'Gray. Wes Gray.'

The sheriff nodded his head. 'Thought it might be. Heard you were up in Palmersville. Some teamsters were talking about you a day or two ago. They couldn't have been describing anyone else.'

'I don't think being sheriff gives you the authority to intercept telegraph messages,' Wes told him.

'Like I say,' the sheriff answered in his slow-talking manner, 'this is my town. I keep trouble at bay any way that suits me.'

'Well that's an important message, Sheriff, and it needs to reach Fort Pierre as soon as possible.'

The sheriff re-read the note. 'Is this true, illicit whiskey among the supplies on their way to the Sioux Agency?'

'It's true.'

'Among the supplies that left here yesterday?'

'That's right.'

'Well that won't look good for us if word gets round that Spearpoint is sending whiskey to the Indians.'

'When the army halts that supply train they might find that whiskey isn't the only problem they've got.'

'I'm intrigued, Mr Gray. Tell me more.'

'No. Send that message to the Commanding Officer at Fort Pierre. It's a government matter.'

'Government! Well, perhaps I can help you there. Come with me, there's someone at the hotel you should meet.' He handed the message form back to the telegrapher with a nod of approval.

Wes Gray hadn't arrived in Spearpoint a moment too soon. The man Sheriff Dix introduced to Wes already had his bags packed and would have left town already if there had been an earlier train to travel on. As it was, as soon as the crew had done the necessary checks, filled the tank with water and had a meal, the train that had recently arrived would be hauling its four carriages and caboose back to Kansas City at which intersection passengers could change to main-line trains for all points east and west.

As far as Wes could tell, the man was around his own age and although he was well-barbered, finely dressed and fleshy about the face and body, he gave

121

the impression of strength, intelligence and good-humour.

'Mr Hunter,' Sheriff Dix told Wes, 'is with the Bureau of Indian Affairs. He came here to supervise the unloading of the cattle and see them off on their journey across the Missouri.'

Rumours of unrest among the Sioux had been gathering strength over the winter and there were grave fears that the warmer weather would initiate an exodus of warriors from the Agencies and hostilities would be renewed. Anxious to prevent an uprising and to prove themselves capable of controlling the situation, the newly formed Bureau of Indian Affairs had posted capable men to the troubled areas to glean whatever information they could about the situation. More than once, the story of infected cattle had reached the Washington authorities.

As a result, Jim Hunter had been sent to the unloading pens at Spearpoint to inspect the latest delivery. He had found no evidence that the animals were anything but top quality beef.

Wes outlined the scheme that had been put in place to switch those animals before they reached the river.

'I scattered the infected cattle last night,' he told the others, 'but it doesn't mean they won't still try to carry through their plan. It might take a couple of days but they'll be able to round them up and drive them on to the Reservation.'

'What will they do with the prime beef?' asked Jim Hunter.

'Cut the government tags out of their ears, rebrand them and sell them on. Could be they'll drive them back into the pens here.'

Sheriff Dix snapped his fingers. 'There's a cattle buyer staying in this hotel. I wondered what he was hanging around for so early in the year. Perhaps he's expecting to take possession of a herd. Let's go and have a word with him.'

The cattle buyer, Ben Warren, was alone and drinking coffee in the hotel dining room when the three-man party caught up with him. He and Jim Hunter had already met, had dined together two nights earlier in company with a common acquaintance. As the holder of the contract for delivering supplies to those Agencies that were situated in the most easterly locations of the Great Sioux Reservation, Jim had sought out John Lord to get his opinion about unrest among the tribespeople. Ben Warren had done business with John Lord in past years, and yes, he confirmed that John Lord was the owner of the herd due in the stockyards any day soon.

'You're not suggesting that John Lord is involved in this swindle, are you?' Sheriff Dix recounted the rancher's high standing in the surrounding territory.

'It's not just the cattle,' Wes explained. 'He's also stealing the goods that are stored in his Palmersville warehouse and sending out shoddy replacements. I thought when the Secretary reformed the War Department it was meant to put an end to the double-dealing that was rife under William Belknapp.'

123

'Those changes affected the traders in the military forts,' Jim Hunter announced, 'but the Bureau of Indian Affairs is determined that corruption will not succeed in their dealings with any of the many tribes that have been forced to abandon their traditional ways.'

Wes wanted to believe the words he heard but he'd heard similar from other men in the past. Jim Hunter might believe what he said but his voice didn't govern the views of the people in Washington. 'There will always be greed,' he said, 'there will always be a need to fight for justice.'

It was agreed that Jim Hunter and Sheriff Dix would ride out after the cattle, would stay with the herd until it was either across the Missouri or under the control of the soldiers sent out from Fort Pierre. Wes, in the meantime, set course for Palmersville.

TEN

The two men that Wes Gray had left trussed beside
Clem Oates's burning body returned shame-faced to
Tad Carter with the news of the scattered herd. By
mid-morning, two riders sent to investigate the possibility of gunfire in the hills, brought back the bodies
of Pecos Tongs and his partner. Tad Carter's angry
outburst hid his fear but couldn't disguise the fact
that he didn't know what to do next. He couldn't stop
the wagons, they had to continue on their way across
the Missouri, but the cattle were a different matter. He
could hold them for a few days while the other herd
was re-assembled, but that could be dangerous and
would generate suspicion; if the army were sent out to
investigate he wouldn't be able to offer an acceptable
excuse. On the other hand, if he drove the animals on
to the Cheyenne River Agency they would lose the sale
to the cattle buyer waiting in Spearpoint, and Tad
wanted his share of the money.

Eventually, he settled for the fact that it was a decision for John Lord to make. He needed to consult

with his boss. It would mean holding up the cattle for a day, but he could ride to the ranch and be back by nightfall. After issuing orders to those who remained with the herd, he set out at a steady pace. He thought about Wes Gray as he rode and the prospect of meeting him face-to-face held nothing but terror for him. The frontiersman had been a menace since his arrival in Palmersville. Five men were dead, cattle scattered and the illicit contents of the wagons discovered. Tad was chilled by the thought that he might be on the trail ahead, heading for a showdown with John Lord.

Wes Gray hadn't beaten Tad to the ranch; in fact he was just on the point of leaving Spearpoint following his talks with Sheriff Dix and Jim Hunter, but John Lord wasn't there either. Accompanied by the Santee Sioux Lame Dog, he had headed for Palmersville earlier that morning. Tad hung about long enough to swap horses then followed his boss's trail. Forty minutes later, his racing entrance into the town drew the attention of the townspeople along the boardwalks. It surprised no one when he hauled his mount to a halt outside the building that was John Lord's office.

John Lord listened to his associate's catalogue of accusations against Wes Gray with growing concern. The message brought by Lame Dog had been unsettling enough; he agreed with Horace Archer's assessment that the man called Medicine Feather posed a greater threat to their scheme than that other meddler, Crackaway. Tad Carter's news emphasized

126

the calibre of his opponent. Although he knew that Wes Gray was just another man, fallible and mortal, the reputation he'd brought with him had been more than justified by his actions. It was clear that Tad found no relish in the prospect of another meeting with the frontiersman.

'What'll we do?' Tad wanted to know, the question aimed specifically at the handling of the herd, but John Lord's brain was considering more that the immediate problem.

'More to the point,' he muttered, as though thinking aloud, 'is what will Mr Gray do.'

'Do you think he'll come here?' asked Tad. 'Come gunning for you?'

'Not straight away. If that had been his priority he'd have been here before you. He had a head start on you, didn't he?'

Tad considered the possibility that Wes Gray was in town, was watching this office and merely waiting for John Lord to step outside. When he voiced that thought, Lord looked to Lame Dog for assistance. The Sioux guard went out the back door. 'If Wiyaka Wakan is in town,' he told John Lord, 'I will find and kill him.'

'What about the cattle?' Tad asked again after the Indian had left them.

'We might have to let them go across the river,' Lord told him. 'We've got to consider what Gray's done with the information he has. If he hasn't come back here seeking answers then we've got to assume that he has passed it on to the authorities.'

'You mean the sheriff?'

John Lord shook his head. 'If he knew that the Bureau of Indian Affairs had a man in Spearpoint he might have tried to contact him.' He paused a moment, mentally weighing the chances of Wes Gray being in possession of that information. To his knowledge, the scout hadn't been to Spearpoint; indeed his name hadn't been mentioned when he'd been at the railhead town a couple of days earlier and the arrival of such a celebrity wouldn't have gone unnoticed. No, he concluded, Weston Gray couldn't have known about the Bureau's interest in the cattle that had been unloaded there. 'Jim Hunter intended taking the first train out after the cattle left the pens,' he said aloud, 'perhaps he's already gone.' He pushed concern for interference from the Bureau of Indian Affairs to the back of his mind. 'If he found the whiskey on the wagons then he'll report the matter to the army. If they find it they'll come here to search the warehouse. They mustn't find any of the government supplies. Unload as much as possible on the shopkeeper, anything else you can take to the ranch.'

'What about the whiskey on the wagons? Do you want me to ride back there and have the kegs destroyed?'

'There isn't time for that. We'll deny any knowledge of it. Put the blame on the owners or drivers of those wagons that are carrying it. They are all independent hauliers. I'll tell any investigators that they've done it without my knowledge, abused my trust.'

Tad Carter chuckled. He'd always admired his

128

boss's cool manner, his ability to think quickly in order to gain credit or shift blame.

'Get to work,' John Lord told Tad. 'Tell Hal Adamson he needs to get as much stock into his store as possible, and I want paying for it by the end of the day. Then get the rest out to the ranch.'

'What'll I do for transport? All the freight wagons are on their way to the Cheyenne River Agency.'

'There must be other wagons around. Get what you can. Just make sure that you clear the warehouse of any incriminating stock.'

When Tad Carter had left him, John Lord went to the safe that sat in a corner behind his desk. From it he took several stacks of money, which he then packed into saddlebags that had been stowed away in a tall cupboard. He was wondering if he was overreacting to the recent news; it was possible that Wes Gray had attributed the attack by Tad and Clem Oates to a personal vendetta; that they were seeking revenge for the beating he'd handed out in the saloon. It wasn't even certain that he would report the illicit whiskey to the army. It could be that he'd return to the Cheyenne River Agency and have Horace Archer confiscate it when it arrived. Perhaps he had nothing to fear from the frontiersman, but he wasn't prepared to take that chance.

His immediate plan was to head east to one of the bigger cities where he could lose himself for a few weeks. He had contacts in high places, as high as Washington, if necessary, who would ensure he was cleared of any wrongdoing. It might bring his current scheme to an end but he had no doubt in his ability to find another avenue for making money. He would gather together a few belongings from the ranch, leave some instructions for the running of the place with the foreman then be on the road before night-fall. There was nothing in Palmersville he'd regret leaving behind. At that moment he looked out of the window and saw Jenny Trantor leaving the office of the lawyer, Harry Portlass. Perhaps there was one thing, he thought, and he left his office to follow the girl along the street.

Jenny was feeling happy as she hurried along the town's main street. She had made a decision and final-ized it with her visit to the lawyer's office. She had almost reached the turning that led to her home when she heard the hurrying footsteps behind. Her first thought was that she'd left something in the office, or that Harry Portlass, the lawyer, wanted her to reaffirm what she'd told him. A glance over her shoul-der revealed her mistake and inwardly she trembled when she identified her pursuer. John Lord's atten-tions were unwanted, the more so because of his persistence despite the implacability of her rejection. His need to dominate was apparent every time he spoke to her and it frightened her. No matter how flat-tering his words, he couldn't hide from her the signs of a mean and vicious character.

'Jenny,' he said, catching her arm and turning her so that they were face-to-face, 'I need a word with you.' Jenny tried to shake herself free but the rancher held her tightly. 'I'm heading east for a while. Perhaps

Chicago, Pittsburgh or even New York. It's a trip I'd enjoy a whole lot more if you came along with me. What do you say?'

For anyone else looking at the expression on the face of Jenny Trantor, a verbal answer wouldn't have been necessary. Shocked by his implication that she would ever consider going anywhere with him, her contempt showed in her glowering eyes and tight pressed lips.

'Perhaps we could go and see the Horseshoe Falls at Niagara,' John Lord added.

Jenny was affronted by his arrogance and offended by his disrespect. She slapped him across the face, so hard that it was heard by people on the other side of the street. 'Learn the meaning of the word no,' she told him. 'I will never, ever go anywhere with you. I thought I'd made that clear the last time we spoke.'

The venom in Jenny Trantor's words matched the power she'd put into the open-handed slap and, as a result, John Lord's mouth curled into a snarl, his anger at her apparent revulsion exacerbated by her public act of defiance. He'd retained the grip on her upper arm and used it to pull her a step closer. He slapped her twice using both sides of his hand; hard, nasty blows that were intended to belittle her, to show her and those watching their interplay that she was of little worth. He was the master in Palmersville and wouldn't permit anyone to presume otherwise.

Jenny sobbed with the suddenness and impact of his double strike. She raised a hand but didn't touch her reddening cheek. 'You'll regret that when Mr

Gray returns,' she told him.

John Lord stared at her, the name of Wes Gray prickling fear in him such as he'd never before experienced, but he tried not to let it show. He thrust the girl aside so that she stumbled, bumped against the wall of the bank and fell to the ground. 'Your backwoodsman,' he scoffed. 'If he returns to this town he will be the one to regret it. He'll never get off this street alive.'

When John Lord struck Jenny there had been several exclamations of outrage from those townspeople who were in the immediate vicinity. Some came running to investigate the matter but when John Lord was recognized, many of them held back. The blacksmith, Bob Best had rushed from his forge, a hammer still clasped in his hand. His concern for Jenny's well-being was forestalled by her insistence that she just wanted to return home. Feeling her face swelling and her eyes watering, Jenny hurried away down the alley that led to her house.

'What was that all about?' Bob Best demanded to know.

'None of your business,' retorted John Lord.

'Hitting a woman! You should be ashamed.'

'She deserved it,' was the brazen answer he gave. Looking at the handful of people who had gathered at the spot, his eyes came to rest on Hal Adamson. He singled him out. 'Haven't you got work to do?' he asked the storekeeper. 'Get your stock out of my warehouse and don't dally.'

Hal pulled back his shoulders. 'I told your man, I

don't have any stock in your warehouse.'

John Lord leant forward so that his face was only inches from that of the other man. He spoke softly but with menace. 'I believe we have an agreement.'

Hal Adamson's pale eyes blazed angrily. The day he'd asked John Lord for financial assistance was a day he rued. He'd been forced to accept John Lord's goods ever since, had been made to pay through the nose for them and was no closer to paying off the debt. He wanted to tell Lord that he would no longer buy from him but he knew his business would be sold out from under him if he attempted such a course of action. John Lord had a similar hold over the prices and profits of other traders in the town.

Hal's subservience to John Lord was unknown to his friends and peers, it was a situation of which he was embarrassed; discussing his personal affairs had always been difficult for him. Not even his best friend, Bob Best, was aware that he was in debt to John Lord and it was something of a dilemma. Hal was a town councillor and the council had long been weary of Lord's growing arrogance around town. More importantly his stranglehold on the town's wealth was holding it back from accomplishing its plans. The current amenities were basic and the expectation of financial benefit from the silver extracted from the ground had not been forthcoming. Only the miner's wages were spent in the town and most of those were disappearing into John Lord's coffers. The citizens were still waiting for their new schoolhouse, larger church and better medical facilities. Those were projects that Hal was as anxious to see fulfilled as any other member of the council but knew that they were unlikely to come to fruition until John Lord's domination of Palmersville had come to an end. The fact that that domination had come about because of the weakness of people like himself haunted Hal but more worrying was the knowledge that it would continue indefinitely because no one knew how to break the stranglehold.

Sometimes, in his mind, Hal urged himself to revolt against Lord's orders. He wanted to be strong but knew that he wasn't and when they came face-to-face his determination deserted him. Bob Best's pronouncement that changes would occur if Wes Gray could be persuaded to remain in Palmersville had given him some hope. He wasn't sure what the frontiersman could do or what grounds he would have for doing it, but according to the stories that had circulated since his arrival it seemed that violence was permanently only an arm's length away. If John Lord was killed Hal wouldn't shed any tears; he would be freed from his obligation to the rancher. But Wes Gray had quit the town and there was no reason to suppose he would return. He turned away with Lord's voice ringing in his ears, telling him to get his wagon to the warehouse, and he was aware that Bob Best was regarding him with a quizzical look.

As the people dispersed, Bob Best stood alone on the street, troubled by John Lord's assault on Jenny Trantor and the subsequent outburst against Hal Adamson. In his opinion, the rancher's behaviour had bordered on the criminal, but not only that, it had carried a hint of hysteria. Jenny's slap had, no doubt, been instrumental in inflaming Lord's temper, but it seemed unlikely that that alone could have produced the violent response. What else, he wondered, was troubling the rancher, and how much of it was due to the arrival of Wes Gray in Palmersville? His lips stretched in a grimace, but one which contained a great deal of self-congratulation because he'd predicted an upheaval. He didn't know where the scout had gone but he was sure that he would return and when he did he would be bringing a hornets' nest to slam about the ears of John Lord.

ELEVEN

It wasn't until he neared the outskirts of Palmersville that Wes Gray saw the two flat-board wagons whose dust had been ahead of him for the last mile. If he had caught up with them sooner he might have seen that one of the two horsemen riding alongside the wagons was Tad Carter, but that man had now ridden ahead to report to his boss and left the others to their task at the warehouse.

At Bob Best's stable, Wes dismounted and allowed the pinto to drink from the water trough. He splashed some water over his own face to rid himself of the dust and sweat that had gathered there. He looked down the main street and, in keeping with his first arrival in this town, observed little activity. A disquieting atmosphere hung over the place, as though a great storm was imminent and people had cleared the street to find safety in their own homes. One or two people remained on the boardwalks and Wes could see Sheriff Johnson leaning against a post outside his office. The lawman seemed to be watching Wes, as though his return was likely to be the catalyst for whatever situation was developing.

Despite the sense of relief occasioned by the frontiersman's arrival, the blacksmith was still grim-faced when he stepped outside to greet Wes. He barely looked at the scout, his attention focused on the wagons farther along the alley. They were lined up outside John Lord's warehouse.

'Something's happening,' Bob Best told Wes. 'There's been non-stop activity there since midday. People taking away goods by the wagon-load. Could John Lord be quitting town?' Bob's last words had been barely loud enough to hear, but there was no mistaking that it was an event he wouldn't oppose.

'Who do the wagons belong to?' Wes wanted to know.

'Those two have just come from John Lord's ranch but I've seen some of the town's shopkeepers take away stock. All sorts of goods.'

'Grain? Blankets?'

'Sure. Hal took away a wagon-load to his store.'

'What about whiskey?'

'Didn't see any of that but Benny Kingston at the saloon gets his stock from a supplier in Council Bluffs. He won't deal with John Lord.' The blacksmith shrugged.

'Something wrong?'

'I didn't think Hal Adamson had anything to do with John Lord either, I thought he kept his stock in the other warehouse but he took plenty away from John Lord's earlier.'

'Probably just a business arrangement.'

Bob Best nodded but his face failed to register any sign of agreement. 'It was the way Lord spoke to Hal earlier that surprised me. Ordered him to remove his stock and insisted on payment by the end of the day. Hal was embarrassed but barely raised an argument. Well, he's a good enough man, Hal Adamson, but he isn't a natural fighter.'

From the short meeting he'd had with the store-keeper, Wes had already come to that conclusion.

'Not like your landlady,' the blacksmith added.

'Jenny?'

'Yeah. She had a run-in with John Lord along the street. She slapped his face and he slapped hers.'

'He hit Jenny!'

'Twice. He threatened you, too. Said that if you ever came back you wouldn't leave Palmersville alive.'

Wes ignored that, the only thought in his head was that John Lord had hit Crackaway's daughter. 'Find a shady place for the pinto,' he told Bob, 'I'm going to see Jenny.'

Both sides of her face were still red and a purple smudge was beginning to show along the high bone line of her right cheek. When Wes's gaze settled on it she reached up and touched it gingerly with her fingertips. 'I'm fine,' she said, reassuringly. 'I hit him first. He'd made me so angry. But it won't happen again,' she told Wes, 'John Lord is leaving town. Going east.'

Satisfied that her injuries were slight and that there

wouldn't be any lasting damage, Wes told her what he'd discovered. 'Your father was killed because he'd uncovered a swindle. John Lord is stealing from the Indians and shipping whiskey, which they know will be stopped if their complaints are investigated. I imagine he's also the source of the rumours that threaten war so that no one will listen to their complaints with sympathy.'

'Did John Lord kill my father?' Jenny asked.

'He was certainly responsible for it if he didn't do it himself. But he won't get away with it. The cattle he was hoping to steal will, by now, be heading to the Cheyenne River Agency and I've come back to find other evidence that will lead to his arrest.'

'He threatened to kill you,' Jenny warned.

'Other people have threatened to do that and failed,' he told her, 'but I'll be careful.'

On his return to the main street, Wes found Sheriff Johnson with a shoulder against the same support he'd been using earlier. 'Whiskey is being shipped to the reservation Indians in the wagons that left here two days ago. I expect you'll find more of it in John Lord's warehouse. Proof enough for you to arrest him and hold him until federal authorities arrive with more serious charges.'

Sheriff Johnson rubbed his jaw. 'Perhaps you're right,' he said, 'but I don't have any cause to raid his warehouse. It's only your word against his.'

'You don't have to raid it. They've been shifting stock all afternoon and there are wagons there at the moment. Just watch them.' Wes described the kegs he'd seen on the supply wagon. 'I'm going to Hal Adamson's store to check out the goods he's taken possession of today.'

From his office window, John Lord watched the discussion between the sheriff and Wes Gray. At his side, Tad Carter drew his gun and lined up a shot at the frontiersman.

'Don't be a fool,' Lord told him. 'Do you propose to shoot the sheriff, too? It would be obvious where the shots had come from. Besides, there's no guarantee you would hit anyone at this distance. You need to get closer and pick a spot that provides you with a means of escape.'

They waited for a few more minutes and watched as the duo parted company, the sheriff heading for the far end of the street while the scout walked away along the boardwalk.

'Where do you think he's going?' Tad asked.

'One way to find out,' John Lord told him and with a jerk of his head ordered the other one to follow and kill.

In normal circumstances, the empty street and lack of customers would have been a cause for grumbling, but this day Hal Adamson had other things on his mind. A home needed to be found for the unexpected supplies. His shelves were full and his back room was overloaded with boxes, barrels and bundles. Although he seemed incapable of resolving his storage difficulty he was well aware that the complexity was magnified because his mind was in as great a state of turmoil as his premises. He was ashamed and angry with himself for not responding to John Lord's aggression. He hated the fact that he wasn't a stronger character.

The opening of the shop door and the big shadow that was cast across the floor startled him. Nervously, he looked up and almost croaked a cry of relief when he recognized the buckskin-clad figure who trod softly into his store. 'You're back,' he said.

Wes didn't speak. Instead he wandered around, checking the items on display. He wasn't sure what he hoped to find or prove by inspecting the goods in Hal Adamson's store – he had no inventory to check against, no description of clothing, ironmongery or house-ware that had been despatched from Cincinnati for the Cheyenne River Agency to identify specific items. There was no reason to suppose that anything he saw in the store hadn't been brought in legitimately. There were wool shirts that weren't dissimilar to those he'd seen worn by the Sioux, and denim overalls with bibs that looked familiar but they wouldn't have been out of place in any community. The same could be said of the bowls and drinking vessels he looked at and the kettles and cooking pots, too. None were marked with government stamps or identifiers capable of denoting them as part of a specific consignment.

'Did John Lord supply these?' Wes asked as he examined some thick, grey blankets.

The storekeeper poured out his explanation, relieved to tell someone of his foolishness in borrowing money from the rancher and how he was trapped in an agreement to buy stock only from him. That stock included dry goods but he insisted that the sacks that contained grain, flour and sugar didn't have any marking such as Wes described.

For Wes, if there were answers to be found in Palmersville, they were probably in the warehouse. That, he suspected, was the place where the sacks had been interfered with and where discarded government packaging and labels were most likely to be found. He took his leave of the storekeeper, stepped outside and set course for the warehouse where Sheriff Johnson had gone to watch over the loading of the wagons.

Tad Carter had walked slowly along the main street, looking in the windows of the barber's, the saddle-maker's, the gunsmith's and even the milliner's premises in his search for Wes Gray. Finding him in conversation with Hal Adamson suited his plan. The big store building took up a full block of the street. A tight alleyway separated it from the buildings that housed the barber and the doctor's surgery. An off-shoot from the alleyway gave access to the back of those premises and continuing farther along its length, access could also be gained to the rear of John Lord's office. One shot, Tad reasoned, could put an end to the menace of Wes Gray and an instant later he could be reporting the success to his boss without

142

anyone having grounds to suspect him guilty of the deed. When he observed the frontiersman on the verge of quitting the store he slipped into the alley, drew his gun and waited.

It took a few seconds for Tad to realize that Wes Gray's next destination was taking him to the top end of town, that he wouldn't pass the alleyway in which he was waiting. He edged himself to the corner of the building and peered around the bend. He could see the broad, buckskin-covered back, striding away from him, Gray's long legs taking him rapidly to the extremes of Tad's pistol's accuracy. To get a clearer shot, Tad took a step away from the corner, stretched out his arm and fired.

Hal Adamson's delayed reaction to Wes Gray's enquiry into government markings was probably due to his current chaotic state of mind. Usually, he was mentally alert and quick to make associations, but at present it seemed to take an age for his brain to process information. But no sooner had Wes opened the door to leave than Hal recalled the inventory list he'd found inside a bundle of shirts he'd received from the warehouse some days earlier. There had been something strange about it, something that had hinted that the goods were government issue. He retrieved it from the cash drawer where he'd placed it and followed the frontiersman out of the building. He had raised his arm and was midway through calling Wes Gray's name when the bullet from Tad Carter's gun struck him in the back. With a yell, he fell to the ground.

Cursing because his first shot had failed to take care of Wes Gray, Tad Carter fired again. It was a more hurried effort and consequently less accurate on the shooter's part, but it also missed its target because Wes Gray had reacted with customary alacrity. At the sound of the gunshot he threw himself to his left, rolled on the ground and drew his gun. He could see the wounded storekeeper, half lying on the board-walk, the top half of his body twisted at an awkward angle in an effort to relieve the pain. Beyond Hal, Wes caught a glimpse of a man disappearing into the gap between the buildings.

In an instant, Wes was on his feet, darting forward in crouched pursuit of his assailant. As he passed Hal he could see that the wound was high on his shoulder, hopefully not lethal. He didn't stop; he ran into the alleyway. Although the man had reached a turning that took him behind the main street buildings, he was instantly recognizable to Wes. Tad Carter. He fired a shot which gouged a great splinter from the corner building, but Tad had already made the turning and was out of sight. Wes wasted no time in continuing the chase.

If Tad's ambush had been successful then his plan to reach the rear entry of John Lord's office would have been a good one. In moments he would have reached that haven unobserved and his alibi would have been sound. But failure at the first hurdle had an adverse effect on his escape plan. Once he'd entered the alleyway there was nowhere to hide. Wes Gray was hot on his heels and would catch him or kill him before he was able to reach the sanctuary of the office. He turned to cast a look behind. Wes Gray was in sight and even though Tad fired another shot at him, he continued the pursuit.

The gap between them was closing. Wes would have been justified in shooting Tad in the back – that would have been his own fate if the ambush had succeeded – but he didn't. He called Tad's name and the other stopped and slowly turned. For a moment they looked into each other's eyes then Tad made his move. His arm jerked at the elbow, bringing his hand into a firing position. He was too slow. Wes fired once, the bullet punching into Tad's heart and he dropped to the ground dead.

Not knowing that his enemy had died outside John Lord's office, Wes retraced his steps. On hearing the gunshots, Sheriff Johnson had come running from his position outside the warehouse and was bent over Hal Adamson. The doctor, too, whose office was close at hand was inspecting and tending the wound, telling the storekeeper that the bullet had struck his shoulder blade. 'It'll be painful, Hal, but you'll pull through all right.'

Hearing those words, Wes continued on his way towards the warehouse. He passed Bob Best who was hurrying up the street to acquaint himself with the seriousness of his friend's wound.

Throughout the afternoon, Lame Dog, the Santee Agency guard, had maintained a secret patrol, roving from one end of town to the other, keeping particular watch on the sheriff's office, the saloon and the livery stable at the end of town. Those were the places he expected his enemy, Wiyaka Wakan, to attend if he returned to Palmersville. He was determined to kill the white scout and gain glory and reward for the deed. The first gunshot reached his ears only moments after he'd spotted the pinto with feathers tied in its mane at the rear of the blacksmith's shop. The horse, he knew, belonged to his enemy; it was too much of a coincidence to doubt that the shots had some connection with him too.

Using the fence surrounding the corral in which he'd found the pinto, he climbed on to the roof of the forge then, from there, on to the higher roof of the stable. His perch gave him a view along the main street. His eyes soon fixed on a wounded man lying on the boardwalk. One or two people were hurrying to his aid. Wiyaka Wakan was not among them. The sheriff, gun in hand, emerged from the side street below and hurried to join the growing throng. Another gunshot sounded but it came from behind the buildings on the main street and barely caused a ripple of interest to those treating the wounded man.

Beneath him, Lame Dog saw the blacksmith hurry along the street, as curious as the other citizens to learn the reason for the shooting. He was halfway to where the injured man lay when Wes Gray suddenly appeared. Lame Dog saw the cursory manner in which the scout regarded the wounded man then his brief exchange with the blacksmith before continuing with determined stride in his direction. It crossed

146

Lame Dog's mind that Wiyaka Wakan was coming for his horse.

As he lay on the roof and watched his unwary prey approach, it was clear to Lame Dog that he could kill him with a single rifle shot then disappear before anyone could apprehend him. But he hadn't brought his long gun. He'd anticipated that the killing would be done at close quarters, silently, probably with his knife. He had a pistol strapped to his thigh but he couldn't rely on its accuracy and when he shot Wiyaka Wakan he didn't want him to get up again.

Lame Dog began to shuffle towards the back of the roof where he could overlook the pinto and from where he could launch his attack. A leap from the lower forge roof would have the unsuspecting American at his mercy. There would be none. One powerful strike with his sharp-edged knife would be sufficient to achieve success. Suddenly, he stopped. The scout was not heading for the corral behind the stable; he had turned into the side street from which the sheriff had emerged earlier. Lame Dog looked to his right at the neighbouring flat roofs of the buildings that formed that side street. He judged it prudent to remain hidden until he discovered Wiyaka Wakan's destination, and watching from above might provide an advantage. There were gaps between the buildings but he was confident that he could jump them without betraying his presence. He looked over the edge but his quarry wasn't in view, having moved too close to the building on which Lame Dog stood. A partial shadow, however, was cast which provided the

Santee with evidence of the scout's progress.

Lame Dog set off in pursuit, keeping low to avoid being seen by anyone on the main street who looked in his direction. The first gap required a big leap and he was forced to swing his arms high to gain the necessary propulsion. He landed softly, certain that he wouldn't have been heard by his quarry below.

He was right, Wes Gray hadn't heard anything, but the flap of an inexplicable shadow had caught his eye. A bird, either perching on the roof-line or flying overhead was its logical cause, but when he looked up the sky was clear. He looked back, noted the gap between the buildings and wondered for a moment if the shadow had been caused by something moving from one building to the other. He walked on, curious, wary, on guard. When he reached the next gap he crossed quickly but stopped abruptly and looked back into the space between the buildings. He was in time to catch a glimpse of a dark shape before it disappeared over the edge of the building and on to the roof. Intrigued, and suspicious that Tad Carter wasn't the only gunman who'd been sent to kill him, he decided to become the hunter not the hunted.

In the alley between the buildings an outside staircase led to an upper door. Wes looked up and swiftly calculated that by standing on the top handrail he would be able to reach up to the roof. Cat-like, he hurried up the steps but never took his eyes from the roof edge in case his stalker became inquisitive when he didn't appear at the next gap between the buildings. He climbed on to the handrail, gripped the roof edge and hauled himself up so that his eyes were level with the roof. The first thing he noticed about the man was the red bandana fluttering about the bicep of his left arm. The blue calico shirt and the moccasins on his feet confirmed that he was one of the Santee guards from the Cheyenne River Agency.

Wes's feet found the rail again, giving him a moment to relax his arms then adjust his grip on the roof timbers. Then, with a swift, powerful heave, he pulled himself waist high to the roof then rolled on to its tar-paper covered surface. At that moment he knew that he was seen he was an easy target, and he needed to gain his feet before the man turned around. He failed.

Although he'd followed the ways of the white people all his adult life, the hereditary instincts of a Sioux hunter had not deserted Lame Dog. He turned, startled to see the buckskin figure rolling on to the roof, unsure how his planned ambush had been intercepted but instantly aware of the need to attack if he hoped to achieve a quick kill. He rose, uncaring now if anyone saw him from below, and raced forward.

Wes's worst fears weren't realized. He'd anticipated that the Indian was waiting to shoot him but, as the Santee Sioux came forward he could see that it was a knife gripped in his hand, not a revolver. Wes was on his knees when Lame Dog leapt at him. He grabbed the other's wrist and was able to force aside the plunging blow that was aimed at his heart. Grappling for supremacy, they rolled on the roof. Lame Dog had the initial advantage, the weight of his attack pushing Wes on to his back from which position the scout had to twist and turn to avoid the Indian's onslaught while holding tightly to his wrist to keep the knife point away from his body.

Lame Dog uttered many threats as they struggled and when he worked himself into a position astride Wes's chest it seemed that he would make good his words. But he'd failed to pin down the American's arms and when Wes swung his right arm, his fist connected with the side of Lame Dog's head. As the Indian slumped from the blow, Wes heaved with the lower part of his body throwing the Santee aside. Scrambling to his feet, Wes drew his own knife and both men faced each other in a crouching style, prepared to fight to the death for they both knew that one of them must die.

The commotion on the roof now had the attention of the people below and they watched the bitter struggle that was being enacted. At one moment the combatants were locked together, each holding the other's knife arm then, breaking free, first one would attempt a slash or stab then the other.

The end was not long delayed. Lame Dog, relying on his strength because he was a big man, hoped to take Wes by surprise by launching himself forward and swinging the knife in a vicious arc meant to slice open his enemy's belly. Wes reacted quickly, rocked backwards to avoid his opponent's attack then stepped forward with a thrust that went under Lame Dog's arm and into his heart. The Santee guard staggered against Wes, his head bouncing against the

American's chest as his knees buckled, his knife fell from his hand and his body slumped on to the roof.

Wes withdrew the blade, wiped it on the dead man's blue calico shirt and replaced it in its sheath. He dragged the body to the edge of the roof and tipped it over on to the street below.

TWELVE

Sheriff Johnson tried to restrain his anger when Wes climbed down to the street. Two men dead and the doctor busy digging a bullet out of a prominent citizen was not his idea of a peaceful town, which was his goal. The brutal way the frontiersman had hurled the body from the roof didn't sit easy with him either.

'Who is he?' he asked Wes Gray.

'He's the link that connects John Lord with the Cheyenne River Agency,' Wes replied. 'His name is Lame Dog. He's an Agency guard and I assume he came to Palmersville with a message from Agent Archer. There's a conspiracy to cheat the Sioux on the reservation. The army will soon be riding into this town to arrest John Lord. If you take my advice, Sheriff, you'll put him in jail until they get here.'

As they walked back along the main street Wes explained the situation to the sheriff. Sheriff Johnson was incredulous but was forced to agree that the situation was serious when he learned that not only the

152

army but also the Bureau of Indian Affairs were involved.

'I'm not sure I have any cause to hold him,' Sheriff Johnson said, 'but I suppose there are questions that need answering.'

'Not least of which is why Tad Carter and Lame Dog were out to kill me.'

The lawman had been thinking more about the activity that had taken place at the warehouse which tended to fit in with Wes Gray's claim of double-dealing, but as they had reached John Lord's office he spoke no more about it.

The door was locked. Sheriff Johnson rattled it and rapped on it with his knuckles but without receiving any answer. Wes looked through the window. A door leading to a back room was slowly closing. 'Is there a back door?' he asked, his voice urgent.

Sheriff Johnson pointed to an alleyway at the end of the block. 'Down there,' he said, and when Wes rushed off in that direction, he followed.

Wes recognized the spot as soon as he turned the corner. The body had been removed but this was where he'd had the shootout with Tad Carter. Its proximity to John Lord's office proved to him that the rancher had been instrumental in setting up the assassination attempt that ended in the wounding of Hal Adamson. Any thought of mentioning that to the lawman, however, was instantly banished when John Lord, astride his high black saddle horse, burst out of a wooden stable building directly opposite the rear entrance of his office.

In the narrow alleyway there was little room to avoid the onrushing animal. The sheriff yelled for John Lord to stop but it was clear that the rancher had no intention of obeying the instruction. Instead, he extended his right arm. He brandished a long-barrelled Colt and fired once. The bullet hit the lawman, who spun and crashed into Wes Gray. The pair fell to the ground, the sheriff groaning with pain and Wes struggling to unholster his own gun so that he could return the rider's fire.

John Lord fired a second shot, which struck the wall above the tumbling frontiersman's head and ricocheted away down the alley. Stretching his arm behind as his mount picked up speed, he fired again. The bullet flew high of its mark and Wes, who had now drawn his own gun, was able to send shot at the fugitive before he gained the main street and disappeared from view.

Wes spared a moment to inspect the sheriff's injury. The bullet had entered the right side of his body just above the waist. Wes couldn't see an exit wound but guessed by its downward trajectory that it had lodged against the lawman's hip-bone. 'I'll get help,' he promised as he set off in John Lord's wake. He directed a couple of men to the location of the stricken sheriff and ordered another to find the doctor. His own pursuit of John Lord was too important for delay.

When he reached the blacksmith's shop, Bob Best

confirmed that John Lord had passed by in an almighty hurry only seconds earlier. Wes leapt on to the pinto's back and set a course past the cemetery and on to the range land that led to Lord's ranch. In addition to scanning ahead for a sight of his quarry he also kept an eye on the fresh ground tracks. He'd gone less than a mile before reining the pinto to a halt. Dismounting, he knelt to inspect the dark specks that had begun to show on the ground. As he suspected they were blotches of blood. Either his hurried shot had hit Lord or it had hit his horse. When he rode on, the prints he was following became deeper, an indication that his quarry was travelling more slowly. The blotches were also becoming more pronounced. Whoever was wounded, man or horse, they were beginning to lose a lot of blood. Up ahead, wisps of dust hung in the air signposting the route of the refugee from justice. A mile ahead he'd ridden into an extensive rock formation. Wes pushed on, determined to catch up to the rancher.

It was the pinto, again, that passed on a warning to Wes. They had slowed down to walking pace when they entered high cliffs and boulder land, but the Indian pony stopped suddenly and lifted its head in the unique way it had done on two previous occasions. Wes sat astride the animal for a few silent seconds then, conscious that he provided an easy target for anyone planning an ambush, dismounted. He ground-hitched the pinto then plotted a route that would take him in a high circle through the surrounding rocks.

It was John Lord's black that had been wounded by Wes's snap shot. He hadn't climbed far when he espied it at the other side of the outcrop, behind which he'd left the pinto. The wound was along its flank but the motion of running had sprayed blood all over its rear leg and rump. Its distress was slight and Wes was sure that with proper care it would soon recover. He was more concerned about finding John Lord, wondering if he was hiding somewhere among the rocks, waiting to ambush the next person to ride that way and steal their horse, or if he was continuing on foot towards his ranch house.

He didn't have to go much farther to discover the answer. Looking down, he could see John Lord lying on the shoulder of a weather-formed boulder that overlooked his troubled horse. His rifle was in his hand; he was ready to waylay anyone who should happen by. Wes suspected that John Lord knew who would be first on his trail, and perhaps, looking back, he'd seen his dust when they were still on the open-range land.

Wes descended without displacing the smallest stone, rustling the leaves of the sparse bushes or snapping any of the dry twigs that lay in his path. When he was five yards behind the rancher he removed his hat and skimmed it so that it landed a few feet in front of the rancher's face. John Lord's initial reaction was to tighten his grip on his rifle and half turn to face his pursuer. Then he relaxed, didn't complete the turn, but seemed to address his words to the frontiersman's hat. 'Come to take me back? It won't do any good. I

156

know too many people in high office for anything to be proved against me.'

'The trouble with people like you is that you think the people you know are the only ones in high places. I'm sure they have their own enemies and those enemies will know how to use charges of corruption to topple them. You might find that those friends in high places have already deserted you to protect their own positions. The Bureau of Indian Affairs is hot on your trail, the army, too.'

John Lord gave a short laugh, which was meant to be derisory but only reflected the concern that Wes Gray's words had evoked.

'But you shot Sheriff Johnson back in Palmersville,' Wes continued. 'You'll be in jail for that while the federal charges are being collected against you.'

Again, John Lord tightened his grip on his rifle. The scout was painting a bleak picture. He didn't want to go to jail. If he could ride clear of this territory then he was sure he would be able somehow to turn the situation to his advantage.

Wes Gray was still talking, his voice a deep, threatening monotone. 'Of course, before getting back to Palmersville you have to answer for the death of my friend, Crackaway. You shouldn't have done that.'

The threat in the words and the voice frightened John Lord. He looked over his shoulder. The buckskin-clad figure had adopted a stolid stance; his legs firmly planted, his hands either side of the buckle on his gunbelt. Lord's index finger slipped inside the rifle's trigger guard as he weighed up the odds of

157

turning and firing before Wes Gray could draw his gun.

'And then there's Crackaway's daughter,' Wes added. 'You shouldn't have hit her. I told you Jenny was under my protection. You have to answer for that now.'

The relationship between Jenny Trantor and the old man who'd observed his men stealing from the Indians' grain sacks had little chance to register with John Lord and might have been of no significance if it had. All he really heard was the frontiersman's final word, 'now', and he reacted with the determination of a thoroughbred sprinter to the starter's gun. He rolled, pulling the rifle with him to get it in line with his adversary, his finger automatically tightening on the trigger.

Wes reached for his Colt. Two shots cracked and echoed among the rocks. The rifle slid unfired from John Lord's dead hands.

Wes washed the blood from the black's flank but the animal was limping so he didn't load it with its owner's body. Instead, he slung John Lord's corpse over the pinto and they walked the three miles back to Palmersville.

Wes stayed another night in Palmersville. The injuries to Sheriff Johnson and Hal Adamson were painful but not fatal. Both would recover, although the sheriff would evermore limp and the storekeeper would have difficulty thereafter reaching down goods from high shelves.

When he left, early next morning, Jenny didn't travel with him. The lawyer, Harry Portlass, had proposed marriage and she'd accepted. They were staying on in Palmersville, which Harry believed would develop into a good community. Every good community, he'd assured Jenny, needed legal representation. He'd hung his shingle in the town and wanted his business to develop with its growth. Jenny had struggled for a while with her decision, saddened by the thought that she was not fulfilling her father's dream. The plot of land he'd worked for all his life would have to be resold without anyone of the family ever seeing it.

'I don't think that matters, Jenny. Your pa was striving to provide a home for you when you were a little girl, but you're a woman now. You have to live life the way that's best suited for you. If you want to be the wife of Harry Portlass then that's what you've got to do.'

As promised, he visited Kitty Belton on his way back to the Missouri. Her brother wouldn't be home for another two days. Unlike Jenny, for whom more people and advancements in science and technology were something to embrace, something that might bring wealth and position to her husband, Kitty was nervous of the future.

'Hauling is all that Rafe has ever known,' she told Wes. 'I don't know what will happen if the railway comes this far north.'

'There might be opportunities farther west,' Wes

advised. 'Perhaps Montana where they fell great red-woods. They'll be hauling lumber from the slopes for many years to come.'

'I'll tell Rafe,' she said, 'otherwise it might become necessary for me to return to the job I had before I became an army wife.' She dropped her head, then looked up at him coyly, her big, dark eyes glinting. 'Want to spend a dollar?'

Later, on the banks of the Missouri, Wes rubbed the pinto's muzzle while Black Lance put the canoe in the water and packed Wes's few possessions.

'Yesterday the Bluecoats came and arrested the Agent,' Black Lance informed Wes. 'Will they remain on our land?'

'Only until a new Agent is appointed.'

'Will he also cheat us?'

'I hope not, Black Lance, but I have no say in the matter.'

'It should be you, Wiyaka Wakan. You we would trust.'

'I have another job.' Not for the first time Wes wondered if that was true, if he would get to Council Bluffs and discover that the last wagons west had already gone and that he and Caleb Dodge, the wagonmaster, had outlived their usefulness. Things were changing for everyone. No one could predict the future. He pushed away from the bank and paddled downstream.